Dancer on Hors

By Michael Matson

All this happened long ago at a time when such things were possible. It was a time when many people had adventures themselves rather than watch other people have them on television. Of course there *was* no television. Nor were there computers or even radios. The world has changed in many ways from the world Margaret Duggan first discovered.

When Margaret Duggan opened her eyes and looked up at the round, pleasant face of the midwife who had brought her into the world no one had any idea that one day it would be possible to go to the moon or Mars and discover there were no little green men in either place

Where she first opened her eyes was in her mother's bedroom in a brick-red saltbox home near Chester, Nova Scotia, and it was at that moment, barely five minutes old, that she decided that one day she would run away and join a circus. But there was no hurry. She had other things to accomplish first. Growing up was one of them.

Margaret was aware of the sunlight, golden as the new morning, as it filtered through the room's thin muslin curtains, the dancing motes of dust in the air, the living room beyond the open bedroom door with its two Morris chairs, its black horsehair sofa and its dining table covered with a faded Irish-lace cloth. Adjoining that, she sensed the narrow kitchen with its galvanized tin counter and its sink with the metal hand pump that drew water from the barrels of rainwater stored just outside. She could hear the wash of waves on the nearby shore and, in the paddock behind the house, the movement of horses.

"And what will ye be callin' this darlin' girl?" she heard the midwife ask. And another voice, her mother, she knew, said, "Her name will be Margaret."

Of course it will, Margaret Duggan thought. That's who I am. She closed her eyes and dreamed of all the things she would one day do.

How do I know what Margaret thought and dreamed of lying there in her bassinette and regarding the world for the first time? Well, she told me, of course. Margaret Duggan, you see, was my great-grandmother and all that follows are things she told me when I was a little girl.

I have never been quite sure why it was at that particular time in my life that Margaret decided to share her story with me. Perhaps it was because in that year, 1932, things looked the most bleak. It was the third year of the depression. Many people were out of work and the confidence of the nation was at its lowest. Or perhaps it was because that was the summer of my twelfth year and I was beset with all the fears and insecurities of a girl on the brink of adolescence.

My name is Galen Ferris and I lived at that time with my father William, a pharmacist who worked in the drug store his father owned, my step-mother Audrey and Margaret in a comfortable Craftsman bungalow in Seattle's Wallingford district, within walking distance of the University of Washington where I would one day go to pursue, like my namesake, a career in medicine. But that's another story. This is Margaret's.

Perhaps you will question whether these things really happened. Whether they are simply tall tales made up by an old woman to amuse a child. Certainly, that is what my parents thought, sometimes shaking their heads and rolling their eyes as I, wide-eyed and breathless, repeated some recent story. But perhaps even tall tales have meanings that stay with us long after the telling. I leave to you to decide.

And so, here they are, the adventures of Margaret Duggan, in her own words, exactly as she told them to me those many years ago.

You might think that life in a world without all the modern advantages people have today would have been pretty dull. But it was not. It was, in fact, far fuller and more interesting. And that's precisely because we had no modern advantages.

There were no Tarzan movies to go to, no Guy Lombardo Show or Bing Crosby songs on the Radio, no telephone to call friends and chat for hours. But we had much to enjoy. Oh, life wasn't just a great big bowl of whipped cream and cherries. I don't mean that. There were no grocery stores or department stores, at least where we lived, and my mother and father had to work hard to get the things we needed. Basic things like food and clothing. But there was so much more to life.

Children had toys, of course. My older brothers Joshua and Cally, had tin soldiers which they used to stage elaborate battles with metal cannons and charging horses and waving banners. Both had wooden rifles to ward off pretend Indian attacks and for hunting expeditions to shoot ferocious imagined bears. My older sisters, Kathleen, Erin and Megan, had rag dolls to dress up and play house with and tiny tea sets to entertain imagined ladies at elaborate afternoon parties.

Outside our home we had a whole wide world to explore. We lived close to the sea and we spent hours roaming the shore, building forts from driftwood and learning the ways of the tides and the creatures that lived beneath the waves, the rocks and the sand.

Inland a few miles from our home was a small settlement of Mi'kmaq Indians and we would go there frequently to see their world of wigwams made of spruce and pine and to understand the way they dressed and lived by hunting and raising crops. It was there that I discovered my talent for languages, for I quite easily learned to speak their dialect of Algonquian, although I'm afraid my sisters and brothers never did.

There were forests to explore and wild animals to hunt and horses to ride and ...oh, so many other things to do and learn. Even as the youngest child I shared in all of them. From my first moments in my mother's arms or pulled around our property in a wooden wagon by one of my sisters I was learning and preparing for my life to come. And I never forgot that one day I would join a circus - a really grand circus with elephants and tigers and dancing bears, acrobats, musicians, clowns and - well, we'll get to all of that soon enough.

But first there were our family's horses. I was especially drawn to them because I knew how important horses would be as I grew older. There were two of them: Star, a handsome chestnut with a white mark on his forehead that resembled a star, and Stone, a powerful gray the color of the rocks in the fields that lay behind our home.

I learned to ride almost before I learned to walk and by the time I was eight I had taught them to circle their paddock side-by side almost touching at a gallop as I stood on Star's broad back and somersaulted onto Stone's or sometimes stood with one foot on each of them as they cantered about gracefully.

Rather than dolls and tea sets, Star and Stone became my toys. Nor did I have any desire to dress in the frocks or fussy ribbons my sisters craved, although later on in life I certainly learned their uses.

No, although my mother occasionally insisted that I dress and behave like a girl and my sisters thought me strange, I much preferred the rough denims or canvas pants and loose woolen shirts of my brothers. One cannot, after all, turn somersaults on the backs of horses wearing dresses.

When I grew old enough to work, as we all did, instead of choosing the tasks of women…the cooking, the canning, cleaning, sewing and gardening that my sisters so eagerly took to, I followed the paths of my brothers and began to learn how to hunt and trap game, to fish for cod or trap lobsters aboard my father's boat, The Pride of Galway.

And so I grew and learned until the day arrived when I knew it was time to leave.

How it happened was like this:

There were always winter storms raging in from the Atlantic, battering the coasts of Nova Scotia, just as there are today. Frequently the winds would buffet our home for days, howling like some demented soul around the dormers, shaking doors and windows and sending icy drafts across the wooden floors and into bedrooms. Waves would pound against our shores, destroying themselves in high-flung curtains of spray and casting all manner of driftwood far up on the beaches. Seasonal storms were things we Nova Scotians took for granted, knowing they'd soon pass and life would return to normal.

The storm that arrived in the spring shortly after my 16th birthday was different. It began like all our storms, gusts of wind-driven rain that grew stronger, driving us indoors for safety against flying branches. Early on, father and the boys braved the winds to secure our boat, then returned to batten down our house, fastening shutters, bolting the doors of the stable and henhouse to protect Star, Stone, our cow and chickens.

By late afternoon the sky had turned as black as night and winds had reached gale strength and still continued to grow. By nightfall the storm had become a full-blown hurricane, tearing the shutters from the windows, ripping shingles off the roof, toppling trees and sending splintered tree limbs to crash against our outer walls.

Throughout the night the storm wailed and shrieked, shaking our home and threatening to push it off its foundations. Gradually, with the dawn, the winds diminished. But only gradually. Daylight brought more gusts and driving rain but, unable to wait any longer, my father fought his way to the cove where he and my brothers had secured our boat only to return with the news that the storm had taken it. There was not a trace left. Our family's main source of support was gone!

Much of our home was damaged, as well: windows broken, water soaked floors, roof partially missing. The henhouse was gone, who knows where, but the stable, shielded by our house, was safe as were the horses, the cow and our wagon.

Rain continued for the rest of the day and night but the worst was over. The following morning dawned clear with blue skies. We were alive and that was something to be thankful for but there was so much work to be done! While everyone else began the difficult and heartbreaking task of drying things out and putting back together what could be put back together, I ran to the shore to see if anything of use had been blown in by the storm. Perhaps fish. Perhaps a boat we could repair and use.

There was debris everywhere. Driftwood. Planks torn from other structures. Knotted beds of kelp. Branches. Dead birds. It appeared the hurricane had destroyed everything it touched and I could find nothing to be salvaged. But as I rounded the neck of land that jutted out into the sea from one side of the cove I was stunned to see the wreckage of a large wooden ship, tilted sharply to one side and at rest on the pebbly shore. I had no idea what kind it was but it looked very old and as I drew nearer I could see barnacle-encrusted cannons on its broken deck. It was a fighting ship of some sort, placed as if some gigantic hand had scooped it up from the sea bed and dropped it there for me to find.

There was a ragged hole amidships in the ship's hull, probably caused by the submerged rocks that had sunk it. One mast was broken but two others remained. Portions of the main deck were eaten away by tides and the far deck rail was missing and yet, despite these things, the ship was remarkably well preserved.

Of course I had to explore it.

Entering through the shattered hull, I clambered over a jumble of barrels that, judging from their markings, were the ship's stores: grain, gunpowder, salted meat, drinking water…all contaminated, I was sure, by a century or more beneath the waves. Beyond the barrels was what seemed to be crew quarters and there I discovered a few ancient pistols and a sword, which I took with me. A ladder from this room led upward and, climbing it, I found myself on a main deck strewn with rotted ropes and canvas, broken spars and cannons.

Standing there, bracing myself against the one still-intact deck rail, I wondered if this was a 17th or 18th century British Man of War commissioned to patrol and protect our shores. Was it a French vessel of exploration, blown off course by Atlantic storms? Or could it be a pirate ship caught on the rocky shores of Nova Scotia as it sought a hiding place for its plundered riches?

The severe angle of the tilted deck made walking difficult but by clinging to the rail I was able to make my way over fallen debris toward the raised back portion of the ship, past the wheel and up a short flight of worm-eaten steps to what I guessed had been the captain's cabin.

The door had long since been ripped away by the tides but the opening and the portholes along both sides of

9

the room provided enough dim light to see what was inside. Aside from a writing desk bolted to the floor and a built-in frame that might once have served as a bed, everything had been washed or shifted by the angle of the ship to the right hand wall. There, amid the jumble of rotted cloth, broken furniture, pulped paper that could have been navigational charts, shattered glass, pewter mugs, lamps, a corroded sextant and a brass telescoping spyglass was a plain chest of metal and ribbed wood, about 3' x 2' x 3' in length, width and depth. Time, tide and the devouring sea had battered and eaten away the hasps that had held the lid in place and, when I lifted it, I discovered the answer to my family's future.

The chest held treasure. Gold coins and bars and, mixed in among them, in rotted leather bags, silver coins and jewels, mostly red and green that I took to be rubies and emeralds, but others blue and clear whose names I could not imagine but later discovered were tourmaline, topaz, aquamarine and white sapphire.

Filling my pockets with gold coins and jewels to prove to my family what I had found and taking the brass spyglass, I scrambled off the ship and ran home. There was no time to lose. Although it was unlikely anyone else would find the ship immediately, there was always the risk that someone searching for salvage after the storm would chance upon it.

My father and brothers understood the need to hurry. We hitched Star and Stone to our wagon and all of us, sisters, brothers and parents raced back to the shore.

Even with the eight of us, the weight of the treasure chest was too much to carry and we worked in shifts, carrying the precious cargo to the wagon and then refilling the chest after everything had been transferred

Once that was accomplished, we covered the chest with a tarpaulin we had brought with us and, leaving my father to guard the treasure, the rest of us returned to the ship and searched it thoroughly. In what was probably the mate's or bos'n's quarters we found a skeleton, some poor soul trapped below decks as the ship sank. There were a few ancient weapons and a handful of coins, which we took with us. In the ship's galley we discovered pewter plates, ladles, knives and badly corroded copper cooking pots, none of which we had use for.

Just two nights ago we had lain awake, unable to sleep as winds screamed around us like a thousand devils. Now, unable to sleep from excitement, we sat long into the night, our faces illuminated by lantern light, debating what to do, although we realized there was really no choice. There were no banks here, no way to protect our discovery. The treasure was useless to us unless we moved. And there was no reason to stay. Our house was damaged and would take weeks to repair. Our boat was lost.

The following morning we heaped all our meager belongings and new-found artifacts into the wagon. We covered the tarpaulin and chest with a load of hay, tied our cow to the back and journeyed to the Mi'kmaq village. There, I told our friends about the ship, its salvageable timber and iron fittings, copper pots and its cannon, and gave them our cow.

That done, we turned our wagon toward Halifax, a two day's journey to the north.

Halifax

"Let them gawk," Margaret Duggan thought looking back at the staring crowds along the busy sidewalks of Halifax's Chebucto Road. *"We may look like country bumpkins but we have enough money hidden under this load of hay to buy half the town."*

It was April, 1868. The U.S. Civil War had ended three years earlier with General Lee's surrender at the Appomattox Court House. For the past seven years the merchants of Halifax had grown fat trading everything from food and lumber to arms to both sides of America's Civil War and the town, founded over two centuries earlier by Governor Cornwallis, was wallowing in wealth. But let Margaret tell it:

I had never been in a city or even a large town before and as our wagon clattered noisily over the cobblestoned, surface of Chebucto Road, I stared at the richly-dressed people, the buildings and the shops selling hardware, leather goods, bolts of cloth, men's hats and boots, ladies' finery and...oh, my goodness...so many other things. I wanted to jump down from my plain-board seat and explore everything but I knew there would be plenty of time for that later. First we needed to protect our treasure.

It was not yet quite noon when we drew up in front of The Union Bank of Halifax and my father entered.

Moments later, before the astonished eyes of employees and the bank president himself, we transferred the bulk of our fortune to four large and securely locked steel, safe deposit boxes in the bank's vault. Some gold and much of the silver we kept with us for, in the days ahead, there were many things for which we could need ready cash.

Armed with letters of credit, letters of introduction and directions from the awed but solicitous bank president, we climbed back into our rustic wagon and drove to a stable at the edge of Halifax. There, we made sure Star and Stone were properly rubbed down and well fed and rented a carriage and a matched set of horses more suited to transportation in the sophisticated setting of the city.

How strange it all was! There were a thousand things to do and everything was new! Although we chattered excitedly, all of us remained stunned by our unusual luck, the circumstances in which we found ourselves and our thoughts of the days ahead. Already I could see in the faces of Kathleen, Erin and Megan their fascination with the elegant dresses, polished button shoes and the sometimes flamboyant feathered hats of the women we passed. It would not be long, I thought, until they would be similarly costumed and, I smiled to myself, soon enough they would be thinking less of clothes and more of Halifax's young and eligible bachelors.

I had no such ambitions. At least not immediately. As ever, my thoughts were of horses and elephants, brass bands and acrobats, dancing bears and performing tigers.

And I wondered how our treasure would help me achieve my goals.

In the days that followed, my sisters did indeed get their fine clothes. Peterson's Magazine was all the rage at the time and they learned quickly to appreciate the latest Parisian fashions: tiny hats that they wore tilted forward on their heads, ground-sweeping, ribbon-bedecked dresses with lacy petticoats and soft, gathered bustles. Although I found such finery faintly ridiculous, I couldn't help feeling pleased for them.

Converting some of our jewels to cash, we purchased a magnificent, eight-bedroom Georgian mansion on Barrington Street. We hired two maids, a cook and a kitchen assistant. The home, with its carriage house, rested on two landscaped acres and we hired a gardener-handyman to care for the grounds, Star, Stone and our hired carriage and horses.

Much to my amusement and to their satisfaction, Kathleen, Erin and Megan began to take dance and etiquette lessons and became quite proper young ladies. It was not long before they were "discovered" by young men of all sorts and, although my sisters were attractive, I was not so naïve as to believe they were sought after for their beauty alone. Money may not make a woman beautiful but it certainly adds to her allure. Luckily, my sisters had my level-headed mother to watch over them and discourage the least desirable of their new-found suitors.

Many men, having acquired great wealth, might have been content to devote themselves to a life of leisure but not my father, nor my brothers, Joshua and Cally. They had, like so many of us Irish, lived their lives as fishermen. And in those days fish were plentiful. So much so in fact, that the seas around Halifax were referred to as Talimh An Eisc, Gaelic for The Land of Fish.

Using yet more of our jewels, we purchased a fish market and three fishing trawlers. Joshua and Cally captained two and we hired a well-experience and honest captain for the third. My father assumed management of the market and, steadily supplied by our three boats and other contract fishermen, soon expanded it into the largest and most popular in Halifax.

A year and a half passed. With my family thus embarked on new lives, I found myself free to explore Halifax and follow my own interests as I wished and in my own time. It was while doing this that I met Henry Yeend and became involved in his dreams of flight.

Star and Stone were getting old but still enjoyed playing circus. Perhaps it reminded them of their younger days. Every week I would take them to fields on the outskirts of town and we would canter about for hours, the two of them side-by-side as I stood on their backs and practiced tricks. It was good exercise for all of us.

It was on one of these outings that I noticed we were being watched by an older man who had stopped his buggy by the side of the field. Someone curious, I supposed. That was natural enough. One didn't often see people somersaulting about on the backs of horses. I soon forgot about him and he was gone when we finished.

The following week I noticed him again and, curious myself, guided Star and Stone over to where he sat. He was a large man, well over six feet in height and a bit stout but not as old as I had thought from a distance, although his full beard was streaked with white. He seemed quite embarrassed at my approach but introduced himself as Henry Yeend. He apologized for staring at us and interrupting our exercise but said he was fascinated at my agility and surprised that I was a girl.

Well, that was flattering I suppose, and when he asked why I was doing what I was doing, I explained that I intended to join a circus. Rather than laugh at my ambition, Mr. Yeend confided that he also had an aspiration. He was, he said, an inventor. He had made improvements in the safety of steam engines and developed an efficient internal combustion engine. He had experimented with electricity and radio waves. His current passion, however, was flight and he had invented an elongated balloon with rigid internal ribs that he planned to fly to the great lakes and return.

The problem, he explained, was not the balloon, which he called a dirigible, but a way to propel it and a way to provide for passengers. The engine he had developed seemed to be the answer to the propulsion problem but he had not yet thought of a way to attach it safely. The sort of basket that balloonists used for a passenger or two didn't seem to solve that problem either.

"But what about a boat?" I suggested. "Can your balloon lift a boat?"

"A boat?" He had no idea what I meant.

"If you suspend a boat from your balloon using some sort of harness," I explained, "you could attach a large propeller to the boat and use your motor to push the balloon wherever you wished. The rudder of the boat could be used to alter direction and passengers could ride inside. And there's another advantage," I added with a grin, "if you run into problems over the great lakes, at least you have a boat."

He laughed at that but I could see he was intrigued by the idea. His smile soon faded, however. "It might just work," he said, "but I can't afford to buy a boat. I've spent nearly every penny I have on my dirigible."

I promised him that getting a boat would be no problem, if he took me with him on his voyage.

He immediately agreed and within a day, with my brothers' help, I found a good boat and had it carted to the immense barn Mr. Yeend used as a workshop. We set it up on a sturdy platform with wheels and Henry went to work extending the propeller shaft, attaching his motor and fashioning a large wooden propeller.

While he worked, I gathered the supplies we'd need…food, warm clothing, lanterns, blankets and fuel. Although I did not expect trouble, I also purchased a Henry repeating rifle, a new Colt revolver and plenty of ammunition. We estimated it would take three days to reach Lake Ontario, another full day or perhaps two to explore the other four lakes and three more days to return, although a lot would depend on winds and weather.

The final task was to prepare the device from which to suspend our boat. This was made of sturdy ropes and slipped over the elongated balloon like a harness. It was held in place by sealed rivets that fastened to the dirigible's inner ribs. Eight dangling lines descended from the harness and would be tied, four to each side of the boat, which when we were aloft would rest twenty feet below the dirigible.

Our preparations and tests had taken nearly a month but finally we were ready. At 8am on the morning of September 16th, 1870, my family gathered in the vacant field by Mr. Yeend's workshop to see us off. The dirigible was inflated and the boat fastened securely. I assured my family I would see them in a week or so and we cast off the lines that tethered us to the ground. In the unlikely event that we were forced to land and needed to resupply ourselves, I took along a bit of our Spanish gold, some jewels and a few Canadian dollars. These things I carried in a leather pouch tucked inside my coat and secured by a thong that I wore around my neck.

Slowly we rose into the cool morning sky, started our motor and began to fly.

Ill Wind

Those who have traveled in modern airplanes, skimming over the earth at speeds of hundreds of miles per hour and six or seven miles above everything can only imagine how different things looked to Margaret Duggan and Henry Yeend.

How can I explain the feeling of flying?

It was not as though we moved like birds, soaring, turning and swooping through the sky. How exhilarating it must be to do that, I thought! But for us it was every bit as exciting. We moved slowly, almost majestically over the land. I'm unsure how high we were but Henry said some of the eroded peaks we barely passed over were less than 1,000 feet high. We were close enough to the earth to see individual rocks and trees, to identify the crops and animals in the fields and to see the people who worked there, men and women who stared up at our strange craft in disbelief as we motored overhead.

We passed over forests and lakes, rivers and streams and barren land. Occasionally we sailed over towns and stared down at people craning their necks to understand what they were seeing and where small boys ran after us shouting and waving.

The rudder of our boat acted as I had hoped it would and, with the help of a compass that Henry had installed by the boat's wheel, we moved steadily west and south, following our maps toward the Saint Lawrence River and Quebec City.

As dusk approached it grew colder and we wrapped ourselves in warmer clothes and discussed how we would navigate at night. We decided to take turns of four hours each at the wheel, using a lantern mounted over the compass to guide us. I volunteered to take the first shift and after a meal of mutton stew and bread warmed over the boat's stove, Henry wrapped himself in blankets and withdrew to one of the boat's forward berths.

Night fell and the northern constellations began to show themselves: Aguila, the eagle riding high in the center of the celestial equator; Capricornus, the goat; Cygnus, the swan, the sky above us was filled with glittering light from a million tiny suns.

How marvelous and mysterious it all was!

As I steered our unlikely craft westward I couldn't help feeling the awe that the first sailors must have felt, leaving land and venturing forth on the unknown sea. I felt I couldn't sleep if I tried but when Henry relieved me four hours later I fell into a berth and, exhausted by the day's excitement, slipped immediately into a deep and dreamless slumber.

It was sometime after four in the morning that the weather began to change. Wisps of clouds like torn fabric drifted across the sky, hiding, then revealing, then hiding the stars. Soon all celestial light had been obscured and we sailed on in a sea of darkness, unable to see in any direction and only guided by the light of the lantern hung over the compass.

The southerly breeze that had brought the clouds gradually increased in intensity, at first making it difficult and then impossible to keep our craft on course. This was not a storm such as the one that had cast the treasure ship up on our shore but more like a large, steady hand that pushed against us, forcing us farther and farther to the north. Since it was useless to try to steer against it, we decided to cut our engine and save our fuel. We would wait the wind out, take our bearings by the light of the approaching day and get back on course then.

It was a reasonable plan but the wind had other ideas. That day and night and for the following two days it pushed us steadily north until, sometime during the third night it stopped abruptly almost as though it had decided that this, wherever this was, was exactly where it wanted us to be.

As the feeble light of day fought its way through low gray clouds that morning we woke to discover that one of the dirigible's mooring lines had slipped loose during the night and was now tangled hopelessly in the branches of a tall fir tree. The boat itself was lodged in the same tree forty feet above snow-covered ground. We were in a forest at the edge of an immense gray sea that stretched away to the east as far as the eye could see.

Obviously, we had to cut the snagged mooring line but it was apparent that that by itself would not be enough to free us. The boat and its harness were also entangled in the fir's branches and everything had to be cleared away before we could continue our voyage.

Henry was good at many things but clambering about in tall fir trees was not one of them. Together, we sliced through the mooring line and I climbed out onto the branch on which the boat, which had embedded itself bow first, rested. Several smaller branches held it in place and several more were entangled in the dirigible's harness. By climbing from limb to limb I was able to free the harness, then descended to the boat's bow and cleared away the branches there. Finally, I positioned myself precariously in front of the boat with my back against the trunk of the tree. I pushed as hard as I could and was totally surprised when the boat suddenly and easily skidded backwards. Unprepared for how easy it was, I fell, only catching myself at the last moment by throwing my arms around the branch I was standing on.

As I scrambled to regain my feet, I watched in dismay as the boat floated free and began to rise into the sky. Henry raced to the stern and attempted to start the motor but it refused to turn over. Realizing I was stranded and it might be impossible to get back to me immediately, he dashed into the boat's cabin and emerged seconds later with blankets, food, my rifle, pistol and ammunition. These he threw over the side of the boat then rushed back to the motor and tried to start it again.

Again it failed. Caught in an updraft of wind from the sea, the dirigible drifted farther and farther away and I, helplessly clinging to the branches of the tree, could do nothing but watch until it disappeared behind the roof of the forest.

Wolves

My brothers, Joshua and Cally, were the tree climbers in our family and fir trees are not like maples or elms with branches close to the ground that make climbing easier. Nonetheless, I managed to slip, slide and tumble my way to the snow-covered forest floor.

The things that Henry had managed to throw from the boat were widely scattered and it took some time to retrieve everything and gather it in one spot. That done, I wrapped myself in a blanket, leaned back against my fir tree and considered what I should do. The logical thing was to follow the shore of the sea toward the south hoping to find some settlement or town and I had just decided to do that when I got that prickly feeling you get when you think someone is watching you.

Turning my head slowly, I scanned the forest in front and to both sides. There was nothing. No noise. No movement. And yet the feeling persisted and, warily, I turned to look behind me. There, lying belly down in the snow not ten feet away and staring at me was an enormous gray wolf. Without looking away, I fumbled for my pistol, forgetting that it wasn't loaded. As I did, the wolf was joined by two others, equally as large, that flopped down beside their companion.

What were they thinking? That I was some unfamiliar kind of animal? That if I moved they would pounce on me and tear me apart? That I looked like dinner?

If I could find my ammunition and load my pistol maybe I could kill one and frighten the others away.

Keeping my eyes on the wolves, I searched through my cache of supplies and had just put my hand on my box of ammunition when a man stepped out of the forest and walked to the wolves. His sudden and unexpected appearance was such a shock that instead of feeling relief, I simply gaped at him. He was tall, well over 6', with broad shoulders. His eyes were blue and his hair was long and blond. A short, trimmed mustache and beard graced the lower part of his face. He held a long bow in one hand and on his back he wore a quiver of arrows while, across his wide shoulders he carried the carcass of an immense deer as easily as another man might carry a small child.

It was his clothing however, that most startled me. It was not Indian or European but something far older and more exotic. On his feet were sturdy fur-lined boots into which were tucked loose-fitting, heavy-woolen trousers in a dark gray and blue plaid pattern. He wore two tunics, the inner one seemed to be made of coarse un-dyed wool and the outer, which was sleeveless and made of deer hide reached almost to his knees and was held in place by a leather belt with an ornate silver clasp in the shape of a dragon's head. Beneath the inner tunic was a shirt dyed a deep red. Metal clasps in the shape of entwined snakes rather than buttons secured the sleeves to his thick wrists. On his head was a leather, fur-lined helmet vaguely conical in shape and reinforced with vertical metal bands.

Without speaking, he stopped behind the wolves and dropped the dead deer to the ground. He cocked his head slightly to one side regarding me and, I imagine, found me, wrapped in my blanket under a tree, just as odd as I found him. Strangely, none of the wolves acknowledged him as he squatted, crossed his arms over his knees and continued to look at me.

This was eerie. But for some reason I didn't feel threatened.

"Who are you?" I said, breaking the silence. "Are there others here? A town?"

He said nothing.

"Can't you speak?" I demanded. "Do you understand me?"

Still nothing.

I pointed to the wolves. "Are they yours? Are they dangerous?" At this he stood, hoisted the deer to his shoulders and began to walk away.

"Wait!" I cried.

He paused, looked back and said, "Faljga."

I had no idea what that meant but the wolves immediately jumped to their feet and trotted after him.

Well, I was not going to be left there alone. I hastily gathered my few possessions and followed the wolves.

Mortality

For that entire day we trekked inland, sometimes through drifts of knee-deep snow that left me gasping with effort while my guide appeared indefatigable, striding along effortlessly as though he was out for a Sunday stroll.

As it grew darker the temperature dropped and by the time we stopped for the night to share a meal of his deer meat with cheese and bread from my supplies, I had to wrap myself in both my blankets to keep my teeth from chattering. My silent companion showed no sign of being cold and after eating, lay down by our fire and fell asleep.

It grew colder and I wondered if, even with my two blankets, I could survive the night. I needn't have worried however. As soon as I lay down and covered myself, two of the wolves joined me, one on either side, and snuggled up like affectionate puppies. Cozy and comforted, I drifted off into a deep and dreamless sleep.

Sometime during the night it snowed and I awoke to find myself and my two bed warmers covered like a cake with an inch of white frosting.

After a brief breakfast of the last of my bread and cheese we set off again. The morning passed as had the day before, my silent guide setting a steady pace through dense forests under gray skies until, about midday, we reached a broad expanse of broken boulders and shattered rock. This field of stone stretched on all directions for nearly a quarter of a mile, its surface tumbled and fractured as though pounded by giant hammers. On the barren face of this inhospitable plain, frozen snow drifted like windblown sand and, strangely, clouds of steam rose here and there through fissures in the rock. Several minutes after beginning to cross this expanse of stone we came upon a cleft in the stone perhaps 20' across and so deep I couldn't see the bottom.

Since it barred our progress, I expected we would have to find a way around it and I began to look about, examining the surrounding frozen stones for a likely path. When I turned back, my companions had disappeared. I rushed to the edge of the crevasse and saw them descending along a narrow, dangerous-looking trail that seemed to have been formed by the separation of the rock above it. As quickly as I could I scrambled over the lip of the crevasse and followed.

For much of the next hour we wound down through the rock on a trail that grew increasingly dark, narrow and twisted, sometimes so restricted that by holding my arms out to my sides, I could touch both sides of the passage. Gradually however, the way widened and became lighter until, passing through a final series of switchbacks, I found myself standing in brilliant sunlight looking out over an impossible valley: impossible because it simply could not exist. Above us had been deep, unexplored forest, gray snow-laden skies, bitter cold and frozen stone. Here everything was green and as warm as a day in springtime. A road led from the trail we had descended to a wood bridge over a broad, clear-running river, on the far side of which was a compact town of gaily-painted wooden buildings and homes. Beyond the town were vast fields of what looked like wheat and meadows dotted with flocks of sheep and bordered by a large lake. In the far distance and to the right and left, the valley was circumscribed by dim, rocky cliffs similar to the one through which we had just passed.

There were people in the street and more came out to watch us as we crossed the bridge and entered the town. Most, but not all of them, were tall, blond and blue-eyed and dressed in similar fashion, the men in knee-length belted tunics of lightweight wool dyed in a variety of colors and loose trousers, some plain, others in plaid patterns of purples and reds, browns and blues. The women wore lightweight belted smocks of fine wool in widely different colors, their hair hanging in long braids or plaited in coils about their heads and held with silver combs

As we reached the town's main street a tall, handsome woman stepped forward and my companion handed her the deer which she slung over her shoulder and carried off as easily as I carried my blankets. People crowded around us and began talking and gesturing at me. I had no idea what they were saying but they did not seem hostile or unfriendly and I could only guess that they were asking questions. Certainly I could understand their curiosity for I had questions of my own. Who were these people? How did they get here? How was it possible for this valley to exist? What language were they speaking?

I would find out soon enough. But not before I was allowed to clean myself from the trip. I was taken to the home of the woman my guide had given the deer to, provided with soap, a basin of warm water and clean clothes. Through hand gestures, pointing to myself and saying my name, then pointing at my hostess, I learned the woman's name was Hallveig. With more pantomime of bows and arrows, wolves and antlers, which sent Hallveig into fits of giggling, I discovered my traveling companion's name was Skopti.

After that, communication bogged down and we simply sat, smiling at one another and waiting for whatever next would happen. The door to the house had been left open and I could see that even more people had gathered outside and most had taken seats on the ground, also waiting but for what I had no idea.

Perhaps half-an-hour passed when I noticed a short, good-looking, dark-haired man hurriedly threading his way through the seated crowd, most of whom nodded and smiled at him as he passed.

He entered and stopped uncertainly a few feet from where I sat. For a moment or two he regarded me nervously then, very carefully and slowly said in a thick Scottish accent "Do ya no speak English, then?"

His name was Edward Douthett and, after asking me my name and how I came to be here, he turned to the crowd and explained to them what I had said, an explanation that evoked excited reactions and much discussion.

As to my questions…I can only say that the story he proceeded to tell was truly amazing. At times his accent was so thick I had difficulty understanding but slowly, as he spoke, I became accustomed to it. I will not try to duplicate it but only repeat what he said.

"Probably you have heard of Leifr Eiriksson, the Norseman, a man you and I would call a Viking," he began. "Nearly 900 years ago he sailed west from Iceland and landed somewhere in what is now Newfoundland, Canada. He established a small outpost, then sailed home with tales of rich furs, abundant wild game, delicious wild grapes and plentiful salmon.

"His tales excited those who heard them and twenty families, fifty-six people in all, decided to follow his voyage and see this marvelous new land for themselves. They set out in longboats bringing sheep and cattle with them and eventually they reached Canada but, failing to find Eiriksson's settlement, they continued sailing north and west and before long entered Hudson Bay, the great body of water you thought was a sea. It was winter when they arrived and for months the families lived along the shore not far from where Skopti found you.

"That winter was hard. The cattle were eaten, some people fell ill and many sheep died, yet thirty-two people, men, women and children survived. When spring came they began to explore inland and after nearly another year they discovered this valley. They have lived here ever since."

"So these people are the descendants of those early settlers," I said.

For a long moment, Edward looked at me as if trying to find the words to explain. "Well, yes," he finally said. "Most of them are. But not all. Almost all the original thirty-two are still here."

"Here?" I echoed. "You mean buried here in the valley."

"Oh, no," Edward shook his head. "They are all very much alive."

"But that's impossible!" I cried. "Why, they'd be over 800 years old!"

"How old do you think I am?" Edward asked.

My eldest brother, Joshua, was twenty-two and certainly Edward looked no older. "Twenty-two or twenty-three," I ventured.

"Yes," he said. "I was twenty-three when they found me, sick and dying on the shore of Hudson Bay and brought me here. I was a fur trapper and my canoe had capsized in rough water. I lost all my furs, my traps, rifle and supplies. That was 130 years ago. As difficult as it is to believe, I was born in 1713 on a sheep ranch near the fishing village of Kyle of Lochalsh in northwestern Scotland. I think that makes me 156 years old."

The Valley

My parents had been silent before now. But when I ran to my step-mother with the information that there was a secret valley in Canada, filled with Vikings who lived forever, she stopped darning the stockings she was working on and stared at me.

"Galen," she said, "you really mustn't believe everything Nana says."

"But why?" I asked.

"She's a very old woman," was the stern answer. "And we all love her, of course. But sometimes very old people don't remember things well or as they really happened and so they make things up."

I knew this wasn't so. Margaret Duggan's stories had to be true. Even so, I didn't argue. That wasn't the end of it, however. That night after my father came home, after dinner and when I was tucked in bed, supposedly asleep, I overheard my parents talking. I heard, "Margaret," and "lies."

Quietly, I slipped out of bed and crept to the bedroom door so I could hear more clearly. Their voices seemed to be coming from the dining room.

"You have to do something, William" my step-mother's voice said. "She's filling the child's head with nonsense."

They're just stories, Audrey," my father said. "I can't see what harm they do."

"The trouble is, Galen believes them. You need to speak to your grandmother."

"I don't know what good that would do," came my father's voice, somewhat fainter as though he had moved away toward the living room. "You know how strong willed Margaret is."

My step-mother's voice followed. "Well, I think she's losing her mind. Maybe it's time we considered putting her in a home where she can get help."

The voices grew even more muffled and I could make out nothing else although I stayed crouched by the door of my bedroom for several more minutes.

They wouldn't do that would they? Put Nana in a home? Because she wasn't crazy. Her stories were wonderful. I loved them not only for what they were but because of the way they made me feel. They were adventures that I had only before thought of happening to boys or men… to strong self-confident people. But Margaret Duggan was a girl, a woman. Her adventures made me believe that it was possible for other girls, certainly myself, to be as strong and resourceful as she was.

No, I assured myself. Margaret Duggan was not losing her mind. There was a secret valley. I wondered where it was, how it could exist and why it never had been found.

"Well, I'll tell you," Margaret began when I asked. I didn't tell her about my parents' conversation. And later, I didn't have to.

Edward Douthett explained that vast thermal springs lay beneath the entire valley. They provided hot water that kept the year-round temperatures always close to 70 degrees.

"There must be some chemical in the water, too," he said. "Something that prevents aging."

"But why hasn't someone found this place?" I wondered.

"I've wondered that myself," Edward said. "What Skopti says is that the hot springs surround the valley, too. He says they create clouds of steam that cloak the valley from sight."

"But there are blue skies," I said, pointing up. "And sun. If there were clouds wouldn't they hide the sky?"

"I know," Edward admitted. "I don't understand it. Some of the people here believe the valley is hidden by a cloak of invisibility. But they're very superstitious. They still believe in their old gods…Odin, Frigg, Thor, Tyr and Loki."

"And people never leave?" I asked.

"Some do," he said. "Hunters like Skopti and his wolves, leave for short periods."

"No others?" I persisted

"Yes. A few. Over the years some have left and not returned. And others have left and found their way back many years later. When they do they are no longer young. They have aged. You'll see them here, the old men with white beards, the women bent and wrinkled. But the odd thing is, after a while even they begin to look and act a little younger, less bothered by the aches and pains and illnesses that older people often have."

"And what about you?" I asked. "Have you never thought of leaving?"

Edward was silent for a long time before answering. "Yes…I have from time to time. But the world beyond this valley is a hard place. Not hard to make a living in. I am not afraid of that. But there is cruelty, sickness, poverty. Believe me, I have seen it all before. Here there is peace. People are kind. There is no sickness." He hesitated. "I think if I had something I wanted to do badly enough or someone I had to be with, I would leave. But I don't. And who doesn't enjoy being young and full of energy all the time. I grew up on a sheep farm and here I work with the flocks, so I have work. I keep busy."

"I do have something I must do," I said. "I can't stay." And I explained that my destiny was to join a circus."

Edward smiled. "Well, there will be time enough to leave in the spring. Don't forget, winter comes early to this part of Canada." He gestured to the surrounding cliffs. "Any day now the snow up there will be over your head and you'd freeze to death before you traveled a day."

Skopti

The next half year passed quickly. I have always been one to keep busy and I spent much of my time learning enough of their language to communicate with the people of the valley and I helped Edward with the sheep. Not that he needed my help but I enjoyed his company and listening to his tales of the past century.

Life had been hard in Scotland and he had left home at 17 with not much more than the clothes on his back and an old flintlock rifle his father had used in the Jabobite struggles of the late 17th and early 18th centuries. He had made his way across Scotland to Dundee where he was lucky enough to find a ship to the new world willing to take him on as an unskilled seaman. Arriving in New York, he jumped ship and made his way to Ottawa where he worked doing day labor until he had enough money saved for some meager supplies…a few traps, some warm clothes, powder and ball and a good knife.

On his 19th birthday he struck north and for the next four years worked as a trapper-hunter, selling his furs to Hudson Bay Company traders. His goal was to establish his own trading post and each year he managed to save a bit more until, by the spring of 1736, he felt he had enough to realize his dream. Loading everything he had in his canoe he headed south along the shore of Hudson Bay. On the second day of his journey he fell ill. For several days he ran a high fever, losing track of where he was and eventually he capsized his craft. He

*remembered nothing more although he must have
floundered ashore somehow where he collapsed and
certainly would have died if a Viking hunter had not
found him.*

*It was hard for me to imagine Edward living such
a solitary and rough life for he was a born talker,
someone who my dad would have said had, "kissed the
Blarney Stone." He had the gift of gab and a natural
affinity for people. Beyond that he was exceptionally
clever, forever coming up with new ways to improve the
lot of those around him and I found myself becoming
more and more fond of him.*

*I soon became aware that he was growing fond of
me too. But more of that later.*

*I had Edward to talk to, sheep to tend to and
language to learn but I was still restless and so I set about
persuading Skopti to let me accompany him and his
wolves on his hunting trips to the outside world.*

*Convincing him was no easy task. At first he said
I was too young and weak. That I'd never be able to keep
up with him. After I challenged him to a footrace and
beat him by several yards he claimed that it would be too
cold for me, the snow too deep, and he'd have to spend all
his time digging me out of snow banks.*

*A week later I presented him with two pairs of
snowshoes I had made from bent willow branches and
strips of deer hide. With those, I explained, there would
be no need for either of us to worry about getting*

stuck…and besides I was lighter than he was and far less likely to get bogged down.

He still resisted until I promised to show him how to use my Henry Repeating Rifle. Even then he scoffed, bragging that his longbow was all he needed to bring down even an angry grizzly and the rifle was just something extra and unnecessary to drag through the snow. Nonetheless, I could see he was interested and one afternoon he and I hiked to the far end of the valley, he with his bow and arrows and I with the Henry. I had practiced the day before, sighting the rifle and was satisfied it was accurate.

I had found the dried skull of a sheep on the same day I tested the rifle and now brought it along as a target. This I set up on a small rise 100 yards away. I then challenged Skopti to hit it.

I have to admit he came remarkably close. His longbow was an amazing weapon requiring immense strength and concentration to draw and steady. All three of the arrows Skopti let fly landed within two feet of the skull, one less than five inches way and all close enough to hit a deer or an elk.

The area I had selected for my contest had a stream running through it with several birch trees growing along its banks. I congratulated Skopti on his marksmanship then braced the Henry against one of the birches to steady it, sighted and slowly pulled the trigger. The shot hit the skull squarely, shattering it into a dozen pieces. With that I turned to a startled Skopti and handed him the rifle. "It's yours," I said, "if you take me hunting with you and show me how to use a bow."

First Hunt

The bow Skopti presented me with two days later was made from a solid piece of ash and, like all longbows, was as long as I was tall. He also gave me a quiver and a good supply of iron-tipped arrows. For the next week, with Skopti supervising, I practiced using a piece of cloth pinned to a bale of hay which I first set 20 yards distant, then 30 and finally at 40 as my skill increased.

By the second week in January I was able to hit the center of the target seven times out of ten. I was ready and three days later we set out, I, wearing heavy wool under a fleece-lined sheepskin tunic and fleece-lined leather boots, Skopti dressed much as I had first seen him with the exception of the Henry strapped to his back next to his arrows.

As Edward had predicted, the snow was deep but it had not snowed for several days and there had been a brief warming spell followed by a hard freeze and now the snow surface was crusted over. Even so, without our snowshoes we could have broken through with every step. I wondered aloud how we could possibly carry any game across this icy expanse. Surely the extra weight of a deer would sink us to our necks.

Rather than answer, Skopti led me to a nearby stand of cedar, broke the crust and scooped away several inches of snow to reveal a sled fashioned from ash and leather thongs. This was about ten feet in length and four feet wide and had a braided rope at one end for towing. When I asked if he always used the sled for winter hunting Skopti replied with a straight face that no, he had just made it to pull me behind him when I became too tired and weak to follow him. I glared at him angrily and he burst out laughing, the first time I had seen a break in his mask of Scandinavian imperturbability.

The more I glared the harder he laughed until finally, gasping for breath, he admitted no, it wasn't for me and yes, when the snow was this deep, he always used it, not only for heavy game but to carry what supplies were needed...food, blankets, cooking utensils...the things required for two- or three-day hunts. Turned upside down and covered with pine or cedar bows it would also provide us and the wolves shelter at night.

But I have forgotten to mention the wolves. Skopti was the only one of the valley's hunters to use them and he used them in an ingenious way. When he discovered signs of deer, elk or moose, he would send the wolves ranging far ahead of us. Hunting in a pack, they would often find their prey more quickly than we could and drive it back toward us until it was close enough for us to be sure of a killing shot.

This method of hunting obviously required a rare degree of communication between man and animal and I asked Skopti how he had trained the wolves and, because I wanted to talk to them sometimes, I asked what their names were. For a moment he looked at me as though I had gone quite mad, then patiently explained as he might to a child that they were wolves, not people, and they certainly didn't need people names. As for training, he said he hadn't trained them, they had trained him. Or rather their ancestors had, so many years ago that he had forgotten who they were. Each generation of wolves Skopti raised from pups and every generation learned to hunt by watching their parents.

I would like to say that my first hunting trip was a success but it was not. In the two days we hunted I had only got one good shot at a deer and I missed. Skopti was more successful, killing an elk on the first day and a large deer on the second. These we butchered immediately before they could freeze. We feed the entrails to the wolves and packed the sectioned meat in snow and stored it on the sled.

Now that I was able to talk to him a little, Skopti was more open and I found him a wonderful, knowledgeable companion. As we returned to the valley I asked him if, in all his trips, he had ever run across others. There were Indians in the area, he said, and he had many times seen signs of fur trappers but he had always avoided any contact.

"But weren't you ever curious?" I asked.

He shook his head. "Of course I was," he said. "But contacting outsiders would be dangerous. They would want to know about me and the people. Possibly they would follow me. If others discovered the valley, our way of life would disappear. People would come. We would have to fight and you have shown me with your rifle that the world has weapons we don't. Even with our skill with the longbow we would be destroyed. Thousands of strangers would seize our valley and lands. And they would keep coming. Think about it. Who wouldn't want to live forever as we do?"

I understood although it was difficult to think about. My destiny from those first moments in my cradle, I knew, was to live in the moment, to fully experience my life and this amazing world. I had no wish to live forever.

As we were returning and drew close to the valley, passing through a stand of frozen birch, we startled a flock of wild turkeys nesting high in the branches. They fled into the sky making their distinctive throat-churning calls, their wide beating wings whirring and clacking like a thousand playing cards caught in the blades of a massive spinning fan. For a moment the sky was full of them and their magnificent noise and then they were gone. The complete silence of a snow-filled world descended on us once again and I could only stand in quiet wonder and admiration at what I had seen.

Leaving

In the months that followed I grew ever closer to Edward Douthett although my feelings troubled me. If my fondness for him continued to increase, how could I bear to leave him?

At the same time I gave serious thought to Skopti's words, "Who wouldn't want to live forever as we do?" At the time I had immediately thought, not I. But as Edward became more and more important to me, I had to consider the idea more carefully. Consequently, I began to study the lives of the people of the valley more objectively: their work, their leisure time, their interactions. It was one thing to say they appeared happy, content. But, I came to realize, there was a terrible sameness to their lives. There was no sense of discovery, of new accomplishment, of new things entering their lives. No invention.

Time for them simply stood still. Each day, each week, each month was the same. True, they were strong, beautiful people but it was as though they were preserved in amber like some perfect prehistoric insect. Like the valley itself, they existed without change. Were they truly happy, I wondered or did they in some barely-understood way feel cursed, blessed with eternal life on one hand, on the other hand too afraid of death to make life significant? Was this what I wanted?

No, I decided. I didn't want to live this way. How much of that decision was influenced by my age I couldn't tell you. I was young, restless and healthy. My life was just beginning. And what young person, still in their teen-age years doesn't feel they will live forever, anyway? I would leave. Even if it meant never seeing Edward again. When the snow began to melt in the world above the valley, I promised myself, I would say my goodbyes and get on with my life.

As fate would have it, however, I had no voice in choosing the moment of my departure.

Skopti had said that there were Indians and fur trappers in the area. On our subsequent hunting trips I too, discovered signs of them; once a trail beaten into the snow by the passage of many unshod horses; another time an abandoned log shelter with a forgotten, rusted iron skillet left behind.

On the day fate intervened, we found ourselves on a mountainside overlooking a vast expanse of Douglas fir. It was early March and there were signs that the hard Canadian winter was relinquishing its hold on our world. There had been no snowfall for several weeks. Ice had begun to break up in some of the larger rivers and some hardy plants had begun to thrust their tentative way up through the snow in areas where the white blanket of winter lay thin. The sun was at our backs, warming our shoulders through our heavy, fleece-lined tunics. The air was crisp and clean and still, the sky that soft, pale blue that acknowledges the sun but retains the feel of winter.

I think we both saw it at the same time: a thick column of smoke rising above the forest less than a mile away.

"What do you think it is?" I asked.

"Probably trappers," Skopti said. "There is a small river near where the smoke is and I once saw a cabin there. I had forgotten we were so close."

I would have loved to investigate but I understood Skopti's fear of discovery and we turned to head back across the mountain to where we had left our sled an hour earlier. The wolves, sensing where we were going, raced on ahead.

Perhaps it was because we were hurrying, our minds occupied, that we didn't see the bear cubs until we were almost on top of them. Skopti, who was about ten yards in front of me, realized immediately what was going to happen and was reaching for the Henry Repeating Rifle when a blur of black tore across the area to my right and barreled into him. Before he could protect himself he was pounded to the ground and the bear was ripping and tearing at his chest and head.

Hoping to startle the enraged sow I ran at her, yelling and waving my arms, but she ignored me. My cries, however, brought the wolves back at a run. The sow left off her attack and reared up on her hind legs looking around for her cubs which had scampered away at the first moment of her assault. Before the bear could drop to her feet and run, the wolves were on her, leaping on her back, lunging at her throat, darting under her blood-stained claws as she tried to defend herself. For a moment she managed to break free from them, dropped to her feet and fled, the wolves in hot pursuit.

I ran to Skopti and attempted to rouse him but it was no use. His throat had been torn open and his life, a crimson banner of death, had bled out into the pristine snow. Horrified, I sank down beside him too stunned to even think. How long I would have remained there without moving I don't know but after some time I became aware of the wolves as they returned, one-by-one. As they did, each paused by Skopti's motionless body and touched it, first with their noses, then by placing one paw on his chest almost as if patting him, as if they were saying goodbye.

Is that what it was? I don't know, but I want to believe that was it, a gesture of respect, a way to pay homage.

Then, as I sat shivering and in shock, each wolf came to me and cuddled close as if in mutual sympathy. How long we remained like that, huddled together and miserable, again I couldn't tell you. But that is how Alain Maigny and Gautier Devereux found us.

Recovery

"I hated telling you of Skopti's death," Nana said, "but it is important to know that bad things happen. Life isn't simply a series of interesting and entertaining events. Both darkness and light exist and one or the other may occur disproportionately in different lives. What you have to understand is that when something awful enters your life you need to work through it. That doesn't mean you can't be unhappy or mourn, simply that as the stale old adage says, 'life goes on,' and you must go with it."

"Even so, it must have been frightening," I said.

"Yes," she said. "But I knew I had things to do."

"What?" I asked. And this is how she continued her story:

It was difficult getting through the days that followed. I mourned Skopti's death deeply and was saddened that I could never return to the valley without revealing its existence to the trappers who had found me. I would not be able to tell the people what had happened and, of course, most of all I would never see Edward again.

Alain and Gautier's first reaction when they discovered me was that the wolves were attacking rather than consoling me and they were preparing to shoot them when I threw myself in front of my friends, arms out-

flung. I spoke no French but, obviously surprised by my actions and shouts, they lowered their rifles. Strangely enough, the wolves showed no fear and made it equally clear by quickly arranging themselves at my side and by baring their teeth that they were prepared to defend me.

Although I was still in shock, I managed to control myself enough to lead the trappers to our sled. We put Skopti on it and, trappers and wolves eyeing each other warily, set off to pull it over the snow a mile or so to the trappers' cabin.

I had no idea how Skopti would have wished to be treated at the end of his life. He had, after all, lived so long that he had probably long since stopped thinking about final acts. A Christian burial in any case was out of the question. The ground was still frozen solid and it was impossible to dig a grave. Somewhere, however, perhaps in Halifax, I had heard stories of Viking funerals, fanciful tales of burning ships set out to sea.

Fanciful or not, I decided that this is what Skopti would have preferred. Except…I had no ship and the ice-bound river that lay just beyond the trapper's cabin was no sea.

Well, you work with what you have.

On the thick ice of the river I built a tall ship of sorts out of brush, fallen branches and logs I cut using the trappers' axe. In this make-believe vessel, the wolves watching from the river bank, we placed Skopti's body and then set the creation ablaze. The resulting fire threw flames 40 feet into the air and burned fiercely for long enough to melt the ice around and beneath it so that all sank below the surface and was carried away by the silent current.

The following morning the wolves were gone. I hoped that they would return to the valley and their appearance would tell the people Skopti and I were dead.

If I told you that Alain Maigny and Gautier Devereux were rough men it would be like trying to explain Genghis Khan simply by saying he was Mongolian. Neither man could read or write either English or their native French, although they both possessed enough simple arithmetic to know if they'd been cheated when they offered their furs and hides to the Hudson Bay Company, for which they worked as agents.

Personal hygiene, like reading and writing, was another mystery to them. In the fall they would sew themselves into a fresh set of long underwear. This would be worn under heavy wool shirts, jackets and pants with, as the weather became colder, fur being added as required for warmth. During the first warm week of May and sometimes as late as June, they would peel themselves to the skin and take their yearly bath. For the following three months it was possible for strangers to be in their company without gagging. For the rest of the year it was advised by those who knew and did business with them to move hastily to an upwind position.

Of course they ate with a knife and fingers. Of course they never shaved. And of course their cabin was an accurate reflection of themselves, as dark, cluttered and foul smelling as a dead boar's den.

For all of that they were hardworking, honest and kind in their own way. Their occupation had accustomed them to death. They understood grief and treated me with respect. Which was not to say, with kid gloves. After allowing me a few days to mourn, they made it clear that if I was going to stay there and eat, I would have to work.

If, because I was a girl...a woman in their eyes...they expected me to clean and cook for them, they were to be disappointed. I had no intention of playing Snow White to their Seven Dwarfs. Skopti had taught me to hunt well and this was how I earned my keep. There was plenty of wild game in the area and I became adept at supplying my hosts with a steady menu of fresh venison, rabbit, wild turkey and ptarmigan.

I did clean one corner of the cabin, hanging a tattered blanket in front of the skins I slept on to provide myself with a little privacy, but that was the extent of my domesticity. If Alain and Gautier regretted the form of my contribution to their lives, they never mentioned it. In fact, I'm sure it soon became apparent to them that, by relieving them of the necessity to hunt, they were free to devote more time to their trap lines and preparing their furs to sell.

Sometimes, no matter how much you want to do something, the world intervenes. I was anxious to leave but the frozen branch of the Nelson River on whose banks the trappers' cabin stood, was only slowly beginning to

55

thaw. Snow still lay deep throughout the surrounding forests.

I had no choice but to abide by the world's decision. I hunted. I waited.

Fort Garry

Winter that year was particularly severe but by the second week in May the ice-bound Nelson River had cleared. For several weeks prior Alain and Gautier had been preparing their furs and hides for their annual trip to the York Factory, the Hudson Bay Company's headquarters on the south shore of Hudson Bay.

Since my arrival we had painfully worked out a rough system of communication involving hand gestures and a few words of French, English and Cree and now they urged me to accompany them. My destination lay in the other direction, however, and on the 20th of May they departed without me, their separate long canoes piled with the results of their months-long work.

They left behind a small canoe. Or rather the wreckage of one. Its framework was intact but its birch bark skin was broken and rotted through in several places. This I repaired, replacing the rotted areas with fresh-cut birch bark. Over the new skin I stretched dressed deer hide treated with pine pitch and tallow to prevent leakage. The final result was far from a work of art but it was watertight and, I hoped, safe enough.

The trip south was not so much an adventure as tedious. The small river where the trappers had built their cabin fed into the Nelson and it in turn fed into a huge lake. This, I later learned, was Lake Winnipeg, one of the largest freshwater lakes in Canada. 256 miles long, its eastern shore was mostly dense forest consisting of pine, cedar, hemlock and spruce interspersed here and there with birch and aspen. The western shore was more varied with occasional sandy beaches and limestone cliffs many of whose sheer faces were pocketed with caves, which I was in no mood to explore. I had had quite enough of things that lived in caves.

Although my progress was steady I found it slow going since the Nelson River flowed north toward Hudson Bay and I realized why Alain and Gautier had elected to go in that direction rather than south.

In all my eighteen years I had never been so completely alone for such a prolonged period of time or without some specific immediate task to accomplish. Of course I had a goal but now there was mostly nothing to do but paddle and think. No sound but the rush of the water, the whisper and splash of my paddle, the infrequent cry of a bird or of some other animal. On one or two occasions I thought or imagined I saw smoke, perhaps from a cabin or camp, but I saw no certain sign of other humans.

Since the first moments of my life I had been aware of my destiny but I had never paused long to consider who I was. Now, as the long days passed and while I had ample time to reflect, I realized my life so far had been as haphazard as pieces of a jigsaw puzzle put into a sack and shaken. There was a picture to be made of these pieces and I needed to begin.

Who was I? I asked myself. Well, obviously someone with sufficient self-confidence to create the future I envisioned. I understood that gender was no impediment; that anyone could reach for the stars if they but had the will to do it.

I appreciated life. The beauty of the land. The physical joy of work and accomplishment. And, I realized, I loved people. My times with my family, William Yeend, the people of the valley, Skopti, Edward Douthett...even the rough-hewn, odoriferous trappers had been special.

Above all, I decided, I felt comfortable with myself. And so the days passed.

At night I camped along the river or while on the lake at one of the sandy beaches. I fished using hooks I fashioned from deer bones. Several times I camped for a day or more and hunted.

My only fright came one night at dusk. I had pulled in to one of the sandy beaches close by a particularly steep cliff dotted with high caves, established my camp, built a fire from driftwood and had begun to gut and clean the trout I had caught earlier in the day. Suddenly there was a startling susurration of wings overhead accompanied by piercing, rat-like shrieks. Throwing myself flat onto the sand, I looked up to discover the darkening sky filled with a beating, darting, twisting river of bats. Astounded by their sudden appearance, I watched as hundreds, perhaps thousands, poured forth from the mouths of caves. Like a vast black tide they blotted the sky and passed over me to the lake. There their river broke apart as they fled into the night in search of insects.

I have never been fond of bats. I think of them as flying rats and find both rats and bats hard to love. On following days I made sure my camps were located a sufficient distance from caves.

I had hoped to find a settlement of some size at the end of the lake. Instead I discovered an immense marshy delta, miles across and cut by dozens, perhaps hundreds of streams, false rivers and bays with low scattered islands, inland ponds and small lakes. This entire vast marsh was rich with beaver, otter and muskrat. In the thick reeds scurried a world of other small animals and in the shallows and ponds I observed blue and white heron and countless waterfowl. Unfortunately it was also home to swarms of mosquitoes so thick and persistent I was forced to cover all but my eyes to keep from being bitten to death.

Below the maze of the delta the Red River twisted and turned like a tormented serpent through land that gradually began to display signs of civilization: scattered homes set well back from the flood-prone banks, farmland, grazing livestock. I was still a full day away from anything that could be called a large settlement but finally I arrived at the confluence of the Red River and the Assiniboine. There, on one side of the junction stood the walls and towers of Fort Garry, the administrative headquarters of the Hudson Bay Company. Cross river from this sprawling walled complex was a ramshackle settlement of Indians, Métis, fur traders, mule skinners, British, American and French adventurers, shopkeepers, prostitutes, whiskey peddlers, saloons, gamblers, hotels, faith healers, livery stables, Chinese laborers, money changers and political activists—all dependent in one way or another on the territorial powerhouse lodged behind the walls of Fort Garry.

I had wondered what kind of reception I would receive—an unaccompanied girl dressed in worn Nordic wool and stained deerskin, armed to the teeth with pistol, rifle and longbow, paddling a weather-beaten, multi-patched canoe. I had half expected to stand out, to be some sort of curiosity. In fact, however, I made about as much impression on Garry's diverse, polyglot population as a thimbleful of red dye dribbled into a fifty gallon barrel of water.

I had, along with my Spanish gold and a handful of gems, a few Canadian dollars in the leather pouch I always wore on a thong around my neck. Some of these I used to buy a horse and to rent a room in one of the few hotels clean enough to be habitable.

That done I ordered a meal and hot bath be brought to my room and settled in to ponder what my next move would be.

Dwarf

It is true that horses are not famed for their intelligence. Nonetheless, usually I have found them to be easy to train, affectionate and even loyal if treated fairly. My new horse was a four-year old medium gray mare I decided to name Peggy and for the next two weeks I gradually got her to accept the radical idea that I wasn't just going to ride her in a conventional manner but would, from time-to-time, stand on her rump and turn somersaults.

At first Peggy found this notion too bizarre to countenance and did her best to rid herself of the annoying creature prancing about on her backside. When she finally decided that what was happening was not some sort of devious behavior or torture she stoically came to the conclusion that, strange as it was, it was tolerable. From that point on I believe she actually began to enjoy our daily sessions.

To me they were magic. It had been nearly a year since I had been on a horse and my daily workouts acted like medicine to ease the memory of the bear's attack, the uncomfortable weeks at the trapper's cabin, the long boring canoe ride and the loss of Edward Douthett and the people of the valley.

Training brought me peace although I was not unaware that the atmosphere of Fort Garry and the rag-tag cross-river community was tense. For 200 years the entire vast drainage system of Hudson Bay had been controlled by the Hudson Bay Company. This immense area, encompassing what is today all of Manitoba, most of Saskatchewan, even part of the United States, wasn't Canada at all, as I had thought, but was called Rupert's Land, named by Charles II for his nephew, Prince Rupert.

Now the Hudson Bay Company was proposing to sell all of its land to Canada. That would mean new surveys would be done, new land rules applied, new laws adopted. The people who had settled here, indigenous tribes, Métis—those of Indian and French descent—and others who farmed and worked the land would have to adapt. Or rather they would have to accept the new order without having a voice in what it would be. No one was going to ask them what they wanted. Canada would just say, "This is the way it's going to be."

The settlers found that unacceptable and many, led by a man named Louis Riel, were at the point of open rebellion,. Tempers were hot and there had already been a number of nasty incidents which had made the undermanned garrison at Fort Garry as nervous as a lonely frog in a pond full of herons.

In what would turn out to be an ill-conceived and disastrous effort to relieve the tension, the administration of Fort Garry decided to hold a three-day carnival. I suppose they imagined that if everyone was being entertained and having a good time people would forget the whole land sale thing and things would run more smoothly. What they overlooked is that people drink during carnivals and that unhappy, heavily-armed, *people, which everyone was, when drunk can become extremely bellicose.*

Nonetheless, booths involving games of skill and chance were licensed, boxing and wrestling competitions announced, shooting contests arranged. A traveling troupe of actor-clowns was summoned from Quebec and horseback racing and riding events were scheduled.

The horseback riding event was scheduled for Friday, the first morning of the carnival and, although I didn't have any need for the prize money being offered, I decided to enter.

Before that, on Thursday evening the hired acting troupe was to put on its first of three performances, a drawing room comedy in French and, since my French vocabulary was limited to the few words I had picked up from Alain and Gautier, most of them curses, I debated whether or not to see it. I had never seen a play, however, and in the end my curiosity won out. In fact I understood almost none of it but I enjoyed it completely due to the comic antics of one of the actors, a bearded, black dwarf listed on the playbill as "Marcel the Butler." He was an accomplished clown and a superb acrobat who kept the rough-and-ready audience in stitches with his teasing of the other actors, his scene-stealing pratfalls and tumbling and his bumbling handling of nearly every item that came within reach. There was virtually nothing he touched that he did not either juggle precariously or spill in the most dramatic fashion, usually with dire consequences for other actors.

*By Friday morning a roughly circular arena on
the eastern edge of the settlement with wooden bleachers
along one side had been built for the horseback riding
event. There was a good-size crowd, I think about 200
people from Fort Garry and the town and there were four
contestants. The program was to start at 11 and I was
scheduled to go third.*

*The first rider was a gambler dressed all in black
from hat to boots on a magnificent black stallion. He had
hired a bagpiper who played a lively version of, "Oh, the
Gypsies, Oh," and the horse pranced to the music keeping
perfect time, two-stepping, backing and twirling like a
Galway gallant dancing a jig. This was followed by a
young, long-haired Métis who set up five plate-size targets
along the far side of the arena and, as he galloped
bareback in a circle, hung on the far side of his ride
beneath the horse's belly and in three turns around the
course shot each of them dead center with a Colt .44.*

*I had tied red ribbons in Peggy's mane and
braided her tail and she looked very pleased with herself.
I had begged a wooden box from the dry goods store in
the settlement and, after setting it up alongside the edge of
the arena, I set Peggy galloping alone in a counter-clock-
wise direction. I allowed her three turns of the circle, just
long enough for the crowd to wonder what was
happening, before I entered running in the opposite
direction. As we met beside the box, I did a handspring
off it, turning a twisting somersault in mid-air before
landing with both feet on Peggy's rump. We performed*

three more turns around the course to wild applause as I did handstands and backward somersaults.

The fourth contestant was a young lieutenant from the garrison but whatever his trick was to be we never learned. He was so drunk that as soon as he entered the arena he toppled from his horse and passed out. But even so he earned a sarcastic round of applause and a few shouts to, "Do it again."

From the applause I received, I expected to win but I was mistaken. The judges gave the prize to the gambler. I tried to shrug off my disappointment but I have to admit I was a bit hurt.

As I led Peggy back to her stable, wondering what I could have done better, I felt someone walking close behind me and, startled, I turned to discover the little actor from the previous night. He stopped immediately and looked up at me. "You really didn't stand a chance, you know," he said. Then, when he saw that his words had made me angry, he held up one small placating hand.

"It's not because you didn't deserve to," he said. "You were far better than the gambler. But the judges were not going to give the prize to a woman, no matter how good you were."

"Thank you, I suppose," I said. "That makes me feel a little better. But not much. Why shouldn't a woman win?"

He gave a small shrug. "C'est un monde d'hommes. May I walk with you for a moment?"

I nodded and started off again with him trotting at my side. "Besides," he added, "the gambler bribed at least one of the judges. Not much but enough. The lieutenant was supposed to win. His father is the garrison commander and if he hadn't disgraced himself by falling on his drunken ass, the judges would have given him the prize no matter what he did."

"How do you know all that?" I said, stopping again to stare at him.

"Sometimes," he said, "a small person can overhear things. I'm often tolerated like a child who couldn't possibly understand what grownups are talking about."

"You don't," I said, "look anything like a child."

"I know," he said with a tug on his beard. "With this I look like a little black goat." Then placing one finger on either side of his head he pranced in a circle looking so silly I had to laugh.

"If you're trying to cheer me up," I said "you're succeeding."

He stopped in front of me. "Good. Because I want you in a good mood for what I'm about to ask."

"And what is that?"

"Join us," he said.

"Your company? But I'm not an actor."

"And we're not just an acting troupe," he said. "The players are part of a small traveling circus waiting for us in Fargo, North Dakota, until we finish here. We have a trained dog act, a strong man, an elephant, three camels and an Arab trainer, a tightrope walker, even two African lions and a lion tamer."

"A circus?" This is what I was looking for. And what a strange place to find it. "But would the owner approve of my joining?" I asked.

The little man made a comical, courtly bow. "Yes," he said. "I would."

Hasty Departure

I had expected Margaret to continue her tale enthusiastically now that she had reached the moment of finding her circus. Over the following two days, however, she seemed pensive and despite my questions hardly spoke at all.

On the afternoon of the third day I discovered the reason for her silence. When I entered her room I found her sorting through her clothing and possessions, placing some of her things on her bed and discarding others. More unusual, she didn't acknowledge my presence. Puzzled, I plopped down in a chair and waited for her to explain.

Finally, still not looking in my direction and continuing to sort through her belongings, she said, "Your mother and father have decided I'm a bad influence on you; that I'm crazy. They are talking about putting me in a home for old people."

"But they wouldn't do that, would they?" I cried. "They can't."

"Oh, I suppose they can," she said, at last looking at me and taking a seat on the bed which by now was covered with clothing and jewelry. "They've told me they are...how did they put it?...looking into it."

"And you'll let them?" I said in disbelief. "No, *I* won't let them. You're not crazy, Nana."

"Who knows," she said. "Maybe I am. In any case there's not much you or I can do to stop them from trying."

At this, I felt my heart break and I began to sob. Nana held out her arms and I ran to her, hugging her close. "There, there child," she said. "They're not going to put me in a home."

"But, but you said," I stammered.

"Do you think after the life I've led I'd allow anyone to stuff me away like some old unwanted suitcase or baby carriage hidden in the attic? I'd rather die than let that happen."

"But what will you do?" I said. "And what about the circus? I want to know all your stories."

"And so you shall," she said. "At least most of them. Tonight I'll tell you what happened next."

"And tomorrow?" I said.

"Well," she said, "we'll see. Tomorrow is a long way off. Now let me see, where was I?"

"Oh yes," she began after a moment's reflection...

My new small friend was Jean Paul Frenac. He had been born in Senegal and was taken to Paris as a young man of 18.

"There," he said, "I was forced to appear wearing a ridiculous tiger skin toga before credulous crowds in a freak show billed as a man who had been cursed and shrunk by a Senegalese shaman. It's really amazing what some people will believe."

Two years later he had been rescued by a Canadian priest who sent him to Quebec and enrolled him in university. There he studied philosophy and joined a local drama club where he perfected his skills of juggling and tumbling and later formed his touring group of actors.

"But why," I asked, "don't you tell people the troupe is yours?"

Jean Paul shook his head. "There are people who would not understand how a black man, especially a very small one, could own anything. It is better that they think of me as a buffoon. Besides," he added with a wink, "I discovered long ago that if people think I'm simple minded, I can get away with an awful lot of things."

I opened my mouth to protest but realized there were still many things I did not understand about the way people thought. In the years ahead I would learn there was much intolerance in the world, that there were many who would always dislike and even fear those who appeared different than they and those who thought or believed in different things.

I held my tongue.

That evening, after their performance, I met the other members of the troupe, two women and three men. Honoree, who frequently played the romantic lead, was the youngest, a beautiful, dark-haired girl just a year older than I. Clarisse, who was chubby, blonde, quick-witted and played older women, was 23. The men, Jacques, Andre and Henri, who was as stout as a barrel, were all in their 20s.

Jean Paul had also offered the trick-shooting Metis, Charles Devenieux, from that day's competition to join the group and he had accepted, so we were now a troupe of eight. Our plan was to leave as soon as the following night's performance was over. The actors and especially Charles Devenieux were nervous, however. That afternoon there had been more than the usual number of drunken fistfights and it was rumored that a Metis had been shot by soldiers. Charles had heard that someone, perhaps Louis Riel himself, the force behind the Metis complaints, had visited and admonished the Metis for allowing the Hudson Bay Company to use the carnival to manipulate them. There were rumblings that tomorrow would be violent.

The rumors were true but the violence arrived sooner than expected. That night there were attacks on the soldiers from Fort Garry. A riot broke out and looters set fire to saloons and shops.

I awoke to sounds of gunfire and someone pounding on the door of my room. When I opened the door I discovered Charles Devenieux, clothes torn and panicked.

"Get your t'ings and meet us at the river," he said. "Jean Paul has decided to leave immediately. And quick," he urged. "Zay are prob'ly goin' to burn the hotel."

I was out of my room in an instant. And just in time. As I ran down the stairs and out of the hotel, a mob with torches attacked the building and, as I looked back while hurrying to the stable for Peggy, I saw flames spewing from the broken front window.

There was a small river boat waiting for us on the Red River. We quickly clambered aboard with costumes and horses and headed south toward the U.S. border. Some days later we joined the circus in Fargo then, by river and overland, we journeyed to Minnesota and set up camp in a small town just outside of Minneapolis.

Training

For the next two weeks we worked to get ready for our first performance as a company. Jean Paul had admired the gambler's dancing horse from my day of competition at Fort Garry and encouraged me to teach Peggy to move to music. He had hired a band and I selected two pieces, "Darling Nelly Grey" and "Soldier's Joy," to work with. Peggy seemed to prefer the fiddles and pipes of "Soldier's Joy," so we practiced mostly with that and before long she was prancing like an equine Fred Astaire.

I wanted to expand my act and, since that required two horses, I bought a matched pair of blacks. I was a bit stumped trying to think up names for them until Jean Paul said, "Well, they're about the same color I am. Why don't you give them Senegalese names?"

He suggested Babacar and Moustapha and that's what they became. Between sessions with Peggy I began to teach them to gallop smoothly side-by-side.

Everyone was busy. Charles perfecting his shooting act, acrobats and clowns working out new routines, the band practicing its music, the lion trainer, who also worked with the dogs, keeping his charges happy and healthy and Jean Paul running everywhere having posters printed, advertising placed in newspapers, costumes ordered and fitted, concessions leased, roustabouts hired and who knows what else. To obscure the fact that he owned everything, he took Henri with him, all dressed up in a suit, tie and hat like a proper business owner, and let him act as a front man. Since Henri was an accomplished actor and with his rather impressive girth stuffed in a serious looking suit and sporting the requisite cigar, people readily accepted him as a successful showman.

Finally, on a Saturday morning in early July we formed up in our entry procession on the outskirts of Minneapolis. Leading the way was the band blasting out its version of "Old 1812." To this, with its insistent drumbeats bolstered by fifes, Jean Paul had added trumpets and the result was spectacular, so demanding and emotional that it sent chills down my back. I came next, right behind the band, wearing a dazzling white costume covered with rhinestones and silver sequins, standing atop a dancing Peggy all decked out in a rainbow of ribbons.

Behind me the clowns, Jean Paul, Clarisse, Jacques and Andre, turned handsprings and ran wildly about honking horns. Honoree came next, dressed in a flowing pink gown and riding in a straw basket on our elephant, Pricilla. As she rode, she tossed handfuls of ten-for-a-penny candy to the children along our route. Behind her were the lions, the camels, the tightrope walker on stilts, the dancing dogs and trainers, Henri dressed as a ringmaster with top hat and whip, Charles, heavily armed and dressed as a wild Indian and finally, the strong man, a massive Englishman named John Simpson who had draped his near-naked torso in heavy chains and painted his face blue. He carried a drum and would frequently beat it and scream, causing the small children in the crowds to hide behind the skirts of their mothers.

How glorious it all was! At once the culmination and beginning of my dream!

In the following four days we put on six shows, one each night with an extra matinee Saturday and Sunday, but I shall never forget the very first performance, the one we put on that day as soon as we arrived at the field Jean Paul had rented and where the roustabouts had already set up our tent. All around it were the stalls of the concessions selling peanuts, souvenir whips and canes, cotton candy, pennants, tin whistles and offering games of chance...penny toss and "knock-the-doll-off-the-shelf."

I would like to tell you that everyone performed brilliantly that afternoon, but I can't. Perhaps they did. I was so concentrated on my own act that I was in a daze as far as seeing others. I remember dancing around the ring with Peggy then introducing my matched blacks, galloping in circles with one foot on reach of their backs, jumping through blazing hoops of fire and turning somersault after somersault.

And, oh! How I remember the applause, the wonderful applause!

The day before our final performance Jean Paul and Henri left to prepare the way for our next downriver stops. On day five we followed, putting on shows in La Crosse, Dubuque, Burlington and Hannibal.

Circuses moving along the Missouri, Mississippi, Ohio and other rivers were not uncommon in those days and the circus itself was nothing new to America. The first American circus had been formed more than 100 years earlier and the acts and performances they provided were primary sources of entertainment. There were other forms of amusement of course, traveling revival shows with their flamboyant, fire-and-brimstone preachers, touring actors, singers and musicians. But the arrival of a circus in a river town was a major event and thousands turned out to see it. Ours was certainly not the biggest company to travel the Mississippi. Many others had trick riders and sharpshooters but at the time I knew of no others that had an elephant that offered rides to children, exotic camels, lions, skilled aerialists and so much more.

We were unique and everywhere we stopped the crowds were enormous.

The Iron Road

It was becoming apparent by the late 1860s that rail travel would open up the west for travelers and companies like ours and Jean Paul was curious to see how easy or difficult it would be to move our animals and equipment by train.

The Hannibal and St. Joseph Railroad connecting those two cities had been completed a few years earlier and, after our shows in Hannibal, Jean Paul booked a special train west. Even though we were a relatively small circus, our animals, wagons, tent, and people took ten cars. The animals and equipment were up front behind the engine and coal car. We had hired a full crew of roustabouts by now and they came next, then a dining car and finally the rest of us.

Jean Paul was nervous about how the animals would act but aside from our elephant, Pricilla, who needed a bit of coaxing to enter her special car, everything went smoothly.

This was my first train ride and, although it was interesting, I have to admit I preferred the freedom to move about and the colorful crowds aboard the riverboats. There, one could walk from deck-to-deck, salon-to-salon, relax in one's cabin, see gamblers and "painted ladies," farmers hauling produce down river and enjoy nightly musicians and entertainers. Even the stops were more engaging. One could stand at the rail watching gangs of black and white stevedores loading and unloading cargo and gaze out over the town where we were docked and imagine the lives of the people who worked and lived there.

It was during this trip west, as we clattered from one dusty little Missouri town to the next, that Charles Devenieux slid into the seat beside me and announced, "I 'ave these idea for une tres bien trick."

"All right," I said. "Tell me."

He pulled a penny out of his vest pocket. "W'ile you ride," he said, "you 'old a penny overhead and I shoot it."

"Are you serious?" I said. "You're not going to shoot my fingers off!"

Charles looked hurt. "Ah, non, mon chere, I would not do that. Only the penny."

"Charles, you are a wonderful shot," I said, "but I don't think this is a good idea. But if you really want to do it, why not use Honoree? She works as your assistant, right?"

"Oui, Honoree is ver' beautiful and she would do these, but she does not know from one end of a 'orse to its tail. With you going 'round and 'round and up and down, the trick would be fantasteek."

"Charles, no," I said.

"Don' worry, mon chere. I will practice."

"No," I said.

I thought that was the end of it but it wasn't. Charles asked me again when we were in St. Joseph, after our performance there. Again, I said no.

Jean Paul's fascination with trains... I swear he was like a little boy with a new toy... prompted him to return to Hannibal by rail. It would have required two trips and been expensive to return the animals and equipment the same way so he had everything but the performers loaded on a Missouri River steamboat at St. Joseph and sent them on to St. Louis that way.

On the train back to Hannibal Charles asked me again. Finally, to get rid of him, I made him a proposition. I drew a picture of a box that could be attached to his horse's back...not Peggy's...I was not going to risk her life for some wild idea. Atop the box was a grooved stick and in the groove was a penny.

"If you can hit the penny 20 times out of 20 as your horse is galloping in a circle, I'll think about it," I said.

"Excellen'," he grinned.

The day after we returned to Hannibal, Charles and I rode out into the country and set up a ring using rocks and branches. What followed was truly amazing. I had seen Charles, who was billed as Shooting Wolf, the name Jean Paul had given his act, cut a playing card held edgewise in half with one shot from 20 yards away. I knew he was an incredible marksman. That day he proved it again, hitting all 20 pennies dead center in 20 shots without even shaking the stick that held them.

That evening on the steamboat to St. Louis we worked out the act with Henri, Jean Paul and Jacques. We decided that at the conclusion of Shooting Wolf's regular act, Henri would announce a new dangerous event. During his announcement, the clowns Jean Paul and Jacques would set up three wooden boxes in ring center, sit down and begin playing cards. Discovering them, Henri would ask them to let him use an ace. After much fumbling and falling about the clowns would pantomime that there were no aces. Angered, Henri would call in John Simpson, our strong man. John would pick Jean Paul up by the heels, shake him and all four aces would fall out of his sleeves. Realizing Jean Paul had been cheating, Jacques would then chase him around the ring hitting him with a soft cloth club.

All this, we thought, would get a laugh and divert the audience's attention while I entered with Peggy.

When the clowns had disappeared, Henri would find the ace of spades, show it to the crowd and then hand it to me. He would then ask the audience if anyone would bet a penny that Shooting Wolf could not hit the ace dead center as I rode around the ring. When someone accepted the bet, I would leap aboard Peggy and gallop around the ring. On my second circuit, Shooting Wolf would fire, I would dismount and walk around the front of the audience holding the card with its hole dead center.

As Henri collected the losing customer's penny,
Charles would approach him and whisper in his ear,
pointing to me. Henri would shake his head and say loud
enough for the crowd to hear him, "No." Charles would
whisper again and Henri would say, "Absolutely not. It's
too dangerous." Charles would whisper again and plead
with his hands. Henri would give in reluctantly, "Very
well, but I will not be responsible if you miss." He would
announce: "Ladies and Gentlemen and little children,
now a feat no one has ever seen before, something so
dangerous that the ladies may wish to shield the eyes of
their children from the possibility of bloodshed. For the
first time Shooting Wolf will attempt to shoot this penny
out of the hand of our gallant, galloping lady, the
magnificent Margaret Duggan."

He would try to hand me the penny but I would
refuse it, shaking my head. We would argue but finally I
would take the penny, mount Peggy and start to ride,
holding it aloft. After a moment though I would change
my mind, dismount and try to give him back the penny.
We would argue again but I would give in and ride. On
my second trip around the ring Charles would fire and
miss.

Pretending to be frightened, I would dismount and
refuse to continue.

Depending on how we judged the crowd's mood,
we decided we could keep the "I won't do this" fight
going for a couple more times or not. Ultimately, of
course, I could continue. Charles would fire again and
hit the penny, which a roustabout had been positioned to

find. He would run with it to Henri, who would present it to the crowd to, we hoped, thunderous applause.

When we got to St. Louis we performed the act on our first night and it went like a charm. From then on it became one of our most popular performances.

Mr. Woodson

It was not unusual to find a half-dozen or more bouquets of flowers in my dressing room after a performance. These were invariably accompanied by notes from men asking me to join them for dinner or hoping to meet me...invitations I had decided early on to ignore. I had no desire for a romantic encounter. The truth was, silly as it seemed at the time since I would never see him again, I still missed Edward Douthett. Besides, I had been cautioned by Jean Paul that in all likelihood, many of the note writers were married men looking for an uncomplicated liaison with a woman who, to their great advantage, was not going to be around more than a few days.

Ignoring such would-be Lotharios was the easy way to get rid of them. Mr. Woodson proved to be somewhat more stubborn. That first afternoon in St. Louis, I had just changed into a comfortable pair of pants and a shirt when someone knocked on my dressing room door. Opening it, I discovered a young boy holding yet another bouquet. There was no note, which was odd, and when I asked who had sent them, he said it was a Mr. Woodson, then added. "An' he tole me he surely would appreciate an answer."

"An answer?" I said.

"Yes'm," he said. "Like if'n ya'll would have dinner with him after your show this even'n."

"Thank Mr. Woodson," I said, "but I never accept invitations from strange gentlemen."

"Oh, Mr. Woodson ain't so strange. He is mighty persistent though. Most likely he'll send ya'll some more of them pretties," he said, gesturing toward the bouquet before he turned and trotted off.

Sure enough, after the evening show, the boy was back with another armload of flowers. This time I told him to suggest to Mr. Woodson that he save his money. I was not going to have dinner with anyone who had not been properly introduced.

That proved to be the wrong choice of words. There was no afternoon show the following day but at noon there was a knock on the door. I opened it and found the boy standing beside a well-dressed, rather good-looking young man, fairly tall with carefully brushed dark hair and clear blue eyes.

"Ma'am," the boy said, "I like to properly introduce Mr. J. Woodson."

I did have to laugh. "You, sir," I said, "have a lot of nerve."

"Yes'm, I suppose I do," the young man said. Then, showing me a wicker basket he had been holding behind his back, he said, "But now that we've been properly introduced, and seeing that it's lunch time, I wonder if you might like to join me for a short picnic by the river."

I suppose I was charmed by his brashness because I agreed on the condition that I could bring along a friend as a chaperone. He said that would be fine and I found Clarisse in her dressing room and persuaded her to accompany us. Mr. Woodson had rented a buggy for the day and we drove to a scenic, shady spot overlooking the Mississippi where we spent a pleasant two hours lunching and chatting.

Mr. Woodson, who said he and his associates had an interest in banking, was familiar with St. Joseph and we chatted a bit about that. He, too, had ridden the Hannibal and St .Joseph Railroad and had a number of interesting observations on the impact of railroads and their growing relationship to banking, especially the sending of payrolls and other valuable items. He was an admirer of horsemanship, having ridden with several fine horsemen during the war and this was, he insisted, the only reason he had wanted to meet me.

Indeed, that seemed the extent of his intentions and we parted feeling, I think, that we had spent an entertaining afternoon in the company of friends.

I did not see Mr. Woodson again and would probably have forgotten our picnic completely if not for what happened two days later. I was walking through the circus grounds when Clarisse came running behind me waving a special edition of the St. Louis Dispatch.

"Look at this," she exclaimed pointing to the paper's screaming headline that read, JAMES GANG ROBS ANOTHER BANK.

Below this extravagance of ink was reproduced a wanted poster with a photo of Jesse Woodson James.

"I think," Clarissa said with a shudder, "we had lunch with an outlaw."

"Yes," I said. "But an honest one. Mr. J. Woodson did say he and his associates had an interest in banking, didn't he?"

Charm

"I want to correct something I told you the other day," Margaret announced one evening. "Remember I said people back then were short on entertainment and were pleased to see us when we came to town?"

I nodded. "Yes, I remember."

"Well," she continued. "Not everyone was glad to see us. There was one group...the good ladies of the town...who always protested our arrivals and tried to keep others from seeing our acts."

"But why?" I asked. "You were providing something new and exciting."

"True, but they didn't see it that way. They felt the circus was connected to hard drinking and thievery, I suppose. That we were immoral and setting a bad example for people. And they were dead set against people like me who performed in, as they put it, 'unladylike garments' in front of men. They felt for sure I was a lost woman, luring poor, weak men into lascivious thoughts. I was a fallen creature, bound for the fiery pits of you know where."

I had no idea what lascivious meant but I knew where the fiery pits were. I nodded as Margaret continued.

"I'm not saying we lost business because of their protests but the women's complaints ate away at Jean

Paul and he scratched around for a way to calm them down a bit. The solution he finally came up with, unfortunately, involved me. What happened is this:"

We were still in St. Louis when Jean Paul came to my trailer one morning, told me he had a carriage waiting and we were going shopping.

"For what?" I asked suspiciously.

"We, ma jeune maîtresse, are going to buy you a dress."

"A what ?" I practically shouted. "I haven't worn a dress since I was five."

"Ah, but now you will," was the answer. "You are going to be our emissary, our ambassador, our sweet voice that soothes the savage hearts of our critics. "

"Emissary?" I said. "Isn't that some kind of bird ?"

"You're thinking of a cassowary," he said. "Now stop joking and hop in the carriage."

There were a number of shops in St. Louis offering women's fashions and the dress we finally purchased, over my continuing protests, was the very latest style: pearl gray and pink with scarlet accents and really quite lovely. Nonetheless I felt ridiculous as I looked at myself in the shop's mirrors while the proprietress fussed over the full bustle and petticoats, tying ribbons and adjusting the billowing, floor-length hoop skirt. Of course the dress wasn't the final word. Jean Paul decided I needed new high-button shoes, a matching cap, handkerchiefs and a pearl-studded string purse.

It was only when Jean Paul felt I was properly outfitted and back at the circus that he told me the rest of his plan. The following morning, he and I were to take a riverboat south to Cape Girardeau, the company's next stop. There, he had already arranged that we, or rather I, would meet with a group of the town's leading ladies and charm them into believing the circus was harmless, educational fun.

Protesting did no good. Despite my assertions that I was no public speaker and couldn't charm a duck out of the water if I had a string tied to its neck, we went.

Getting to Cape Girardeau was no problem. We were met by a dark-skinned servant who delivered us to a big old antebellum home not far from the river. There had been a fierce artillery battle near the town during the war but the home, a huge Greek-columned thing surrounded by massive live oaks and magnolias, had somehow survived. Since Jean Paul was the same shade as the servant, he was relegated to the mansion's kitchen while I was ushered, as nervous as a long-tailed cat in a roomful of rocking chairs, into the presence of twenty of the coldest-faced females I'd ever seen. Ice in the Nelson River looked friendlier.

For the next forty minutes, the ladies rested their fashionable bustles on soft, upholstered chairs, sipping tea and nibbling sweet biscuits while I tried to convince them our circus was full of simple, law-abiding citizens whose only goal was to provide much needed entertainment. I'm not certain to this day that they believed a word I said and, in fact, most of their questions concerned me and why I felt I had to perform tricks on the backs of horses, a compulsion they seemed to find unfathomable.

As we returned to St. Louis, Jean Paul explained their confusion. Ladies of that class, he told me, might be able to speak two or three languages and most likely had attended a finishing school for young ladies where they learned to polish their manners and make bright conversation, but they had no concept of work. Their ambiton was limited to finding a wealthy husband and their idea of adventure was to attend a fancy dress ball.

"It's much the same the world over," he said. "And mostly it's the fault of men who regard women as weak, emotional, illogical and dependent. Sadly, too many women accept those opinions, or pretend to, in order to achieve a successful marriage.

"Having a goal, a burning desire to achieve something worthwhile," he said, "is incomprehensible to them. It's no wonder they failed to understand your ambition."

I doubt whether my meeting with the ladies had any real effect on their attitudes. But we were greeted with somewhat less controversy when the circus arrived at Cape Girardeau a week later and Jean Paul convinced me to repeat my performance as we headed down river to Memphis, Vicksburg and Natchez.

"How the world has changed," Margaret said when she had finished. "Even some prominent physicians back then believed that if a woman was too educated, it would affect her physically and lead to madness. Today, young people...boys and girls both...can pursue an education and their dreams as they wish. And, if they believe in themselves, can achieve great things."

Premonitions

After St. Louis, the circus moved leisurely down the Mississippi stopping for two-day shows at a half-dozen smaller river towns before arriving at Memphis.

It was early-September. Because I was used to a northern climate, I kept expecting the weather to turn cool but it refused to satisfy my expectations. The temperatures in Memphis still reached into the mid-90s daily. Even though it is a river town and one might reasonably expect cooler nights, they too remained uncomfortably warm and muggy.

More than the weather was bothering me, however. Actually, two things. The first was I was coming to believe I had achieved what I had set out to do and what lay ahead held no challenges. I could see months and even years of doing the same thing, perhaps making small changes and improvements in my horsemanship and presentation but still essentially repeating myself. That idea horrified me.

The second thing was, ever since leaving St. Louis, I had been pestered by the notion that there was someplace I needed to be. Someplace other than with the circus. But where? Was it someplace I needed to return to? Or was it someplace I'd never been? And why did I need to be there? The questions nagged at me.

Despite the heat, the Memphis crowds were huge and appreciative and we decided to stay a full week before moving on to Vicksburg, Natchez and finally, New Orleans where Jean Paul hoped to establish a permanent base. Since New Orleans had a large French-speaking population, he hoped also to re-activate the acting company and augment circus performances with contemporary plays.

In the mornings all of us practiced our acts. Afternoons were devoted to housekeeping, washing and repairing costumes and equipment, feeding the animals and resting up for the evening shows. Most of the performers suffered through the heat in their wagons or, even at times, under them in whatever shade was available. Perhaps more affected than others, I would pack a lunch and ride Peggy north along the Mississippi to the edge of a small forest. There, in the welcome shade of River Birch and Yellow Poplar and, if I was lucky, a bit of a breeze off the river I could relax and think.

There was little to disturb me. Perhaps the rustling of a squirrel scampering from one thick-boled tree to the next. The cry of a sleepy bird. The liquid churning of a riverboat's paddlewheel as it beat its way up or down the river. The distant clumping echo of a woodsman's axe. Often I drifted off into a light slumber for a while before waking and heading back to the circus.

It was during one of those moments of dozing that an image came to me of a broad river in winter. Snow lay deep along its banks and skirts of ice formed along water's edge. There was an adobe fort near the river and a steamboat landing, near which were piled barrels, piles of lumber, reels of wire and boxes of goods. Everything appeared so real I felt I could reach out and scoop up handfuls of snow; so real I awoke shivering from the cold. But where was it, and what did it have to do with me?

I had no idea. But when we reached New Orleans I found out.

Voodoo

New Orleans was everything people had told me it would be. A major world seaport for 150 years, it had absorbed the cultures of other countries perhaps more completely than most other cities. Italians, French, former slaves and free blacks, Irish, Germans and Spanish had all left their distinctive marks and contributed to the richness of its architecture, cuisine and ways of doing business. It was the home of adventurers, scoundrels, pirates, musicians, artists and traders, a city of ideas, tradition and energy.

Although we arrived during a period of backlash against the French, and the language was banned from schools, a large portion of the people spoke it and Jean Paul and the other actors were in their element. Establishing their theater proved to be no problem and almost overnight their plays were attracting large crowds.

Between my own performances I wandered the city, enjoying the restaurants overlooking the Mississippi, the shops and the French Quarter with its distinctive architecture...balconies decorated in delicate filigreed designs of cast iron, its streets filled with musicians, dancers and hustlers.

I was not alone in my meanderings. Jean Paul believed the city, despite its charm, was not safe for an unescorted female and insisted that our strong man, John Simpson, accompany me. I believe this was Jean Paul's way of protecting both of us. Only a totally deranged person would dare to physically confront my protective giant. He was however, someone a clever swindler could take advantage of. Because of his massive size, John felt he could handle any and all things that came his way. He was not simple in that regard, simply overconfident and likely to trust others far too much. Who, he reasoned, would dare lie to him? The answer to that, of course, was any con-man in any city he visited.

John, then, provided the muscles and I, the level-headedness needed to keep him from being entangled in misadventures.

I still had no idea where the snowy river was I had seen in my vision. I had mentioned it to several of the other performers but no one had any suggestion about how to solve the mystery until Honoree recommended I ask a Voodoo Woman.

"What in the world is Voodoo?" I wanted to know.

"I've only just heard of it," she admitted. "I think it's like fortune telling only magic. I've heard people here use it to make love charms or charms to protect them against evil. They say sometimes a Voodoo Woman can see things others can't."

"Do you believe that?" I asked.

Honoree shrugged, "They say there are many Voodoo Women here in New Orleans. They use snakes."

Snakes? That didn't sound very appealing. Nonetheless, on my excursions around the city I kept my eyes open for anyone who might practice Voodoo. A few days after my conversation with Honoree, John and I stumbled across a shop in a small alley near the French Quarter. The name etched on the windows said, "Mombo Euprosie." Below that was the painted image of a snake and the message, "Ask Li Grand Zombi."

"What do you think?" I asked John. "Should I try it?"

"Nothing ventured, nothing gained," he grinned.

"And that attitude has never gotten you in trouble, right?"

"Never."

"Never?"

"Well, hardly ever," he admitted ruefully.

I had expected a Voodoo Woman to be dark, squat and sinister, but what you expect isn't always what you get. The interior of the shop was a bit dark but the woman sitting at a table in the center of the room, working over what appeared to be a small cloth doll, seemed disappointingly normal. She was slender and quite beautiful with skin the color of Café Au Lait and dressed in bright Caribbean colors of yellow, green and red.

There was, however, a snake; an evil-looking thing that John later told me was a python. It lay in one corner of the room, not moving, and I guessed it to be about eight feet long and as big around as a man's leg.

The woman looked up and smiled. "Don' be afraid, child," she said. "Nzambi is no evil snake. He is a good loa."

"Loa?"

"What you call a spirit," she said. "Anyt'ing you want to know, you ask Nzambi and he tell you, him."

"How do I do that?" I asked.

The woman turned in her chair, picked up the snake and put it on the table, holding it there with one hand. "Put your hand on Nzambi and t'ink ob de question, you," she said.

Nervously, I stepped forward and placed one hand on the snake. I thought it might be slimy or repulsive to touch but it was not, neither cold nor hot, simply firm and muscular.

For a moment the woman concentrated, then said, "Dat place be far, far from dis place here. De river be de Missouri. Very cold dere an' de place be Montana. Ova dere is where you need to be very soon."

To this day, I have no idea how she knew this but it turned out she was right.

Going North

That evening, after the performances were over and the crowds had drifted back to their homes, I told Jean Paul that I was leaving. He had been such a good friend I hated to go but I knew now my first dream had been fulfilled and it was time for me to discover the next step in my destiny.

Leaving Babacar and Moustapha in Charles Devenieux's care, I booked passage north to St. Louis for Peggy and myself. From there we traveled by Missouri riverboat west and north to Montana.

The trip was not uneventful. The Missouri River can prove to be both perfidious and unruly. Its rapidly moving waters sometimes shift courses, creating whole new vistas and exposing sandbars in uncharted areas on which even the shallow draft river boats can get stuck. Equally treacherous to an unwary or impetuous captain are the toppled and submerged trees that can pierce a boat's hull and sink it in minutes. More than once we steamed past wreckage of vessels like ours and I shuddered to think of the lives washed away forever.

By far the largest danger was the possibility of a boiler explosion. The huge paddlewheel that drove us forward against the swift-flowing river was powered by steam supplied by massive boilers. Too often boilers overheated and exploded setting boats afire and killing passengers. The men aboard our boat took immense pleasure in recounting such disasters as if proving their fear of nothing by their bravado.

A steamboat was, with its crew and passengers, like a small town that inched along the river against the tide at a snail's pace. On a prolonged trip such as mine people became bored, eager for entertainment and sometimes quarrelsome. To alleviate the tedium, the companies owning the boats sometimes provided diversion. On our boat this consisted of a group of musicians and five "working girls" who came aboard at St. Louis and traveled with us as far as Sioux City, where they disembarked to catch a southbound boat and work their way back to their starting point.

There were, in addition to myself, six other women on board. Four of these were married women traveling to meet husbands at Fort Benton, the steamboat's final destination.

The other two were adventurers headed for careers as dancehall girls or as prostitutes in brothels. Along with the five girls from St. Louis, these two provided enough distraction so I was left unbothered by the men. Of course, the fact that I dressed in my normal pants and shirt with a buckskin jacket and wore a pistol strapped to my waist might have had something to do with that as well.

Travel by riverboat was generally peaceful. But not always. The world we traveled through was wild and restless and once we were fired on by Indians. This occurred one afternoon somewhere in Kansas. Suddenly off to our port, or left side, a small band of horsemen, probably a hunting party, appeared. Galloping along the riverbank beside us they let off several rounds of rifle fire amid wild, bloodthirsty screams.

No one aboard was hit and as one passenger later remarked, "They wasn't really tryin' to kill nobody. They was just havin' fun."

In the same spirit of "fun" half the men aboard ran to their cabins and returned with rifles but the Indians already had turned back, probably laughing their heads off. Their targets no longer visible, the men nonetheless fired a few volleys at nothing in particular to vent their frustration and we moved on.

In the main, the men aboard were a sorry lot...whiskey traders or disreputable schemers eager to seek some unspecified fortune in the far north. Not a few of them, I learned from overheard conversations, were ex-convicts or fugitives from one or another misdeed, failed project or broken marriage. Most of the time they passed the days gambling and a great deal of money and cargo in the form of illegal whiskey or weapons changed hands. On at least two occasions during our two-month passage, men disappeared and, rumor had it, they had been caught cheating at cards and left somewhere during the night. Perhaps stripped and stranded on a sandbar or shot and tumbled overboard.

We had just entered Nebraska when we began to see buffalo, immense herds that spread across the face of the plains like a dark, living carpet.

Sighting the animals gave the men another reason to race for their rifles even though the herds were so far away you would have needed a cannon to reach them. Undeterred by distance, the trigger-happy group blazed away with no effect whatsoever and the herds grazed along unconcerned and untouched.

It was hard to imagine that just a few years later those vast herds would be decimated, the great beasts shot for their hides, carcasses left to rot on the sunbaked plains. Now, however, seeing them was like seeing a piece of living history.

When we reached Omaha, I was witness to another phenomenon of the times. Almost a hundred men rushed aboard carrying picks, shovels, pans and packs stuffed with supplies. Gold had been discovered in the Dakotas and the rush was on by the first wave of men whose eyes were wide and bright with thoughts of instant wealth.

They were an irritating, noisome bunch, some from as far away as Indiana and Illinois. Shopkeepers and clerks, farmers, factory workers and idlers, all as full of hope and chatter as crows in a field of ripe grain. A good many of them soon fell prey to the riverboat's gamblers and lost what little money they had. Mostly, it didn't seem to bother them as they continued to dream of riches and when we reached Pierre, in the Dakotas, they raced ashore, a few of the older passengers among them, jostling one another for wagons, horses and mules to take them to the gold fields.

As I stood at the rail of the riverboat watching them, I was joined by one of the gamblers, a sallow-looking fellow with a large mustache, dressed in a black frock coat, white shirt and string tie. For a moment he watched the scrambling crowd on the pier, then spat over the rail and muttered, "Damn fools."

"Why?" I asked. "Because they believe they can strike it rich?"

He shook his head. "No. Because half of them will be dead inside of six months. They're soft. Got no idea what winter is like in the Dakotas. The cold and starvation will finish off a lot of 'em. Indians will kill a good many more. Oh, sure, a few will find gold and a dozen more will try to kill 'em and take it."

He waved a dismissive hand at the would-be miners. "Maybe a handful of all that lot will come back alive with color in their pokes. And like as not they'll lose a good share of their riches drinking and playing cards."

"So you don't have to go running off with them to find gold," I said.

"No, ma'am," he said. "I surely don't. I reckon I'll just wait for it to come to me."

Fort Benton

As we crept gradually north the weather began to change. By October the nights were cool enough to require blankets and the days to require heavy clothing. By mid-November as we finally neared Fort Benton, the farthest northernmost point of the steamboats route, chunks of ice began to appear in the river and the banks were white with fresh-fallen snow.

We arrived at mid-day on a Friday and, standing at the boat's rail as we pulled into the levy, I marveled at how exactly like my vision the town looked. The year was 1872.

Three years earlier, 1869, had brought more than its fair share of busy to Fort Benton. Early in that year the Mullan Road to Fort Walla Walla on the Columbia River had been completed and Fort Benton became a critical way point for settlers heading west to the Oregon Territory. Merchants multiplied like rabbits, providing the travelers with everything from axle grease, canvas and shovels to leather goods, rifles and ammunition, clothing, harrows, grain for livestock, flour, sugar, salt, cured meats and canned goods.

During the same year, the Whoop-up Trail was opened from Fort Benton to Fort Hamilton in Alberta, Canada. This was a trail used by fur traders running illegal whiskey into Canada. Or at least the traders called it whiskey. A vile concoction of cheap whiskey, ginger,

*molasses, red pepper and chewing tobacco, it was known
among the traders as Whoop-up Bug Juice. Another
common mixture by the same name was made from pure
alcohol diluted with water, Hostetter's Stomach Bitters
and India Ink for color.*

*No sane or civilized person would drink this
abominable stuff, let alone offer it to another human
being. Whiskey traders, however, were unaffected by
scruples and motivated entirely by their desire to acquire
buffalo hides and furs as cheaply as possible. This they
did by offering free drams of their Bug Juice to the
Indians they wanted to trade with. When the Indians
were drunk enough, they cheated them out of their goods.*

*There was little law in either Montana or Alberta
and the traders operated openly and virtually unimpeded,
moving guns, ammunition and illegal whisky north and
hides south to the steamships at Fort Benton and then on
to the factories of the east that produced buffalo robes
and coats or used the hides for leather belts for
machinery.*

*There were decent folks in Fort Benton but a large
portion of the population consisted of scoundrels and
degenerates willing to take advantage of Indians and
whites alike. Fights, gun duels and ill-tempered squabbles
were common and earned one section of the town the
name of "the toughest block in the West."*

*The onset of winter had diminished much of Fort
Benton's activity but it was still a thriving location with
sometimes several steamships braving river ice and*

arriving daily and I was concerned about finding a place to live. Luckily, I had become friends with one of the married women on my voyage north. Lillian Mattingly, from Illinois, was the wife of Albert Mattingly, a dry goods merchant who had travelled to Fort Benton two years earlier. Before sending Lillian the money to join him, Albert had established his business and begun building a comfortable home for the two of them and the family he hoped to have. While he waited for Lillian he had lived in a rough wood and sod cabin behind his store and, since his new home now was ready, I was able to rent the cabin from him when I arrived.

When I say the cabin was rough, I mean it made the cabin of my two French-Canadian trappers look inviting. It was built of sod-packed walls and roof over a single room with a dirt floor, one slit window set high in one wall that let in a minimum of light and a door covered with buffalo hide to prevent drafts, although it failed in this more often than not. For furniture I had a bed with a hair-stuffed mattress and two Hudson Bay Company blankets, a table and one chair, a kerosene lamp and a cast-iron stove that was, fortunately, well enough vented that I failed to die from smoke inhalation.

Winter descended on Fort Benton in earnest during the first week in December. Snow fell heavily and drifted to depths of eight feet against some buildings. Icicles as long as four feet in length hung from eaves and temperatures fell to well below zero. Although I hated to contribute to the whiskey traders' success, I bought a buffalo robe for the freezing nights.

To occupy my daylight hours I chopped wood for the stove, fashioned a pair of snowshoes from willow branches and leather thongs and hunted, sometimes riding Peggy, much against her spoiled wishes, into the surrounding country in search of game. The skills I had learned from Skopti returned quickly and I was able to supply myself and the Mattinglys with fresh venison, ruffed grouse and rabbit with enough left over to barter for flour, coffee, salt and kerosene.

Thick ice formed at water's edge along the Missouri and sometimes bitter winds blew across it cold enough to numb hands and noses. Even so the river never failed to fascinate me and I enjoyed walking along its banks marveling at its depth and power; its even, uninterrupted flow; its quiet majesty. Sometimes at night I would walk to its snowy banks and stand mesmerized by its elegance. In the darkness, with its daunting width framed by snow, it sometimes reminded me of a velvet ribbon pressed between the white pages of a book. Other times, as it shimmered with light from the moon or sparkled with the light of distant stars, I could imagine it was an immense, untamed animal on whose proud, smooth back I could stand as easily as I did on the back of a prancing horse.

Christmas passed. The new year began.

Then one morning in January I discovered paw prints in the snow outside my cabin. Later the same day when I visited the Mattingly store, Lillian was abuzz with the news that three wolves had been seen in the town. Townsfolk were of the opinion that the harsh winter had driven them close to town to find food and people were being advised to keep a careful watch on their livestock. I suspected something different and when I found fresh prints beside my cabin again the following morning, I knew Skopti's wolves had found me. Three weeks later in the midst of the worst blizzard of the year....

Margaret stopped in mid-sentence and looked at the clock by her bedside. It was one in the morning and she had talked for five hours.

"Oh, my," she said. "I didn't realize it was so late."

"But what happened?" I asked.

"We have to stop," she said. "Your mother will be furious with me for keeping you up so late."

"But will you tell me what happened next?" I pleaded.

"Of course, but not tonight. Just be sure for now that one adventure ended and another one began," she said. "Now run along. It's time for sleep."

She ushered me out of her room, still protesting that I was *not* too tired to at least listen but she would hear none of it. Moments later I tumbled into bed, thoughts full of wolves, snow and dark rivers. I was asleep as soon as my head hit the pillow. And in the morning Margaret Duggan was gone.

Believe

We reported her missing and the police came of course, asking endless questions for which there were no answers and, ultimately, accomplishing nothing.

All of us were over-wrought, my father smoking and nervously pacing, myself frightened and my step-mother wringing her hands and proclaiming over and over again how unbalanced Nana was, how she had no grip on reality, how she could be wandering dazed and confused through the streets of Seattle, how all of us should have recognized her mental state and had her placed in a safe home long ago.

At last, unable to stand her smug assertions any longer, I screamed at her to shut up. "It is all your fault," I yelled. "If you hadn't wanted her put away, she never would have left." With that I burst into tears and ran from the house.

The following morning a taxi driver was located who told the police he had picked Margaret up at our house late the previous night and taken her to a downtown Seattle hotel. The investigators determined that she had eaten breakfast in the hotel's coffee shop the next morning, then gone for a walk. Eventually someone turned up who had seen her on Seattle's waterfront and who claimed she was talking to a black dwarf, an operator of one of the horse-drawn tourist buggies that, during the summer months, clattered up and down Elliott Avenue from Myrtle Edwards Park to Pioneer Square.

No one had seen her or the dwarf since.

One reads of old people who wander away and become lost. Confused and disoriented senior citizens who are unable to find their way home again, people who tragically disappear and die without loved ones ever knowing their fate. That's what everyone assumed happened to Margaret Duggan. But it is not.

Weeks passed, then months and we heard nothing. Nearly a year had gone by when one day just after my thirteenth birthday a plain, brown-wrapped package with my name on it was delivered to our home. There was no return address. Thinking it was a birthday gift I took it to my room and opened it to discover a faded poster for the Frenac Traveling Circus. Among the acts promised was, "The Amazing Margaret Duggan and Her Dancing Horse." There was a photo of a black dwarf dressed as a clown, another of Margaret balancing atop Peggy and a third of Margaret with a handsome young man. On the back of this one someone had written, "Margaret and Edward Douthett, Big Timber, Montana, 1873."

Beneath the playbill and the photos were a 19th Century Colt revolver, a white costume covered with sequins and a small leather sack, the sort with a drawstring closure. Inside were twelve Spanish gold coins, two large rubies, a red garnet, two emeralds and a note.

"My dearest child," it read, *"I know your parents and others will never believe the stories I have told you, but I know you do believe them so I leave you these mementos with the hope that you will always remember this: There is no need, ever, to live a life without hope. If you truly want something and you believe in yourself you can achieve miracles. Believe, my child, and know I love you."*

It was signed, *Nana.*

That night I slept with the note under my pillow and my dreams took me back to a sprawling farm on the outskirts of Halifax, Nova Scotia. There was a barn and I walked toward it and then around to the other side where, in a wide, stubble-filled field besides stacks of golden hay, I saw a strange balloon-like thing tethered to stakes driven into the ground. Below the balloon, and attached to it by a net of ropes, was a boat and in it stood a stout, middle-aged man, incongruously dressed in a suit and wearing a derby hat. Next to him was a young girl. As I watched, the man loosed the lines holding the balloon in place and it began to rise slowly into the clear, blue Canadian sky.

For a moment I rose with it, moving closer until I could see the delighted faces of the couple clearly. Then gradually, caught by the wind and driven by an immense wooden propeller, the entire apparition began to move away, becoming smaller and smaller until at last it disappeared.

And I knew…that no matter where Margaret Duggan was now, she was safe and off on another great adventure.

Made in the USA
Monee, IL
26 May 2021